THE CEO

SKYE WARREN

CHAPTER ONE
Poor Little Rich Girl

I LEARNED EARLY not to trust men or money. Both of them have a way of disappearing when you need them most. There must have been some hope left, though.

Because it's my stepbrother who breaks me completely.

Salt hits my tongue before the driver opens the door, splashing the sleek leather interior of the limo with watercolor light. This dock homes the most expensive boats in Boston, outfitting them with caviar and champagne before they set sail.

The driver's face is in shadow, sunshine forming a halo around him, but I already know he's expressionless. Like that time I sweet-talked my way into the flight attendant's lounge? He showed up in his black suit and bland smile, having searched the whole airport with security.

Like every part of my father's life, he's cold and predictable and expensive.

Gravel shifts beneath my sandals. I have to

squint my eyes against the brightness. Seagulls swoop above me as I step onto the long deck, searching for their breakfast, completely oblivious to the thud of my heart against my ribs.

I would know which yacht belongs to Daddy even if I hadn't seen it before. It's the biggest one, the best one. The one that gleams the brightest, with *Liquid Asset* in bold letters.

The silhouettes of three people split the sunlight.

Three people, not one. Disappointment hitches my breath. What did I expect?

Last year Daddy's new wife got so drunk she threw her champagne flute in the air. It came down in a splash of pale liquid and bubbling despair. After the steward mopped up the broken crystal, once the wife had gone belowdecks to sleep it off, Daddy sat looking out at the dark sea. I sat beside him. "Why?" I asked, unable to keep the question in. After so many years it came out. "Why do you keep getting married to these people?"

He had been a little drunk himself. Not enough to play volleyball with the drinkware, but enough that his eyes had gleamed with a distant sadness. He pulled me close, and I nestled against him the way I had as a little girl, breathing in the cedar-salt scent of him.

"I love your mother," he said then, present tense. *He loves her.*

There shouldn't have been enough of the wide-eyed little girl inside me to believe it meant my parents would get back together, not after ten years and even more spouses between them. They couldn't even arrange my visits on spring break without an intermediary—me, of course. But maybe some part of me thought there wouldn't be a new wife this year, after that confession.

Well, now I know for sure. There's no chance of them being together, not even in the same room. But it would be nice if Daddy had stopped marrying his way through every divorcée in Boston's upper crust. Like the limo that picks me up from the airport, there's a new model every year.

Daddy smiles at me from the deck, and I can't help the smile that meets his. Can't help the little run I make down the rest of the deck before launching myself into his bear hug. We're far from a happy family, but I always love seeing him. I may be fifteen years old, but the little girl inside me wears pigtails and wants to run to her daddy.

Even if it means putting up with the strangers he marries.

"How's my girl?" he asks, tucking me into his side.

"Sleepy." A guy in a rumpled suit had snored beside me the whole flight, which would have been more annoying if I hadn't swiped his phone and read his e-mail using the plane's Wi-Fi. Someone had a secret girlfriend in New York City. At least she used to be secret. A few clicks had changed that as we were flying over the Atlantic.

Guilt still knots my stomach, but then I imagine my mother as that man's wife. More likely she would be the secret girlfriend. Men shouldn't be allowed to hurt her so much.

"You can take a nap after brunch," says the woman I was hoping wouldn't speak to me.

"Harper," Daddy says, giving my arm a secret squeeze. He's never forgotten the time I yelled, *You aren't my mommy*. Never mind that I was seven years old. "This is Louise Bardot. Louise, this is Harper. Isn't she beautiful?"

I'm surprised I don't get frostbite, that's how chilly this woman's smile is. "Everything you said about her is true, Graham. She's an absolute doll."

"Thank you, ma'am," I say just to see her dark eyes flash with rage.

Daddy's smart enough to run a Fortune 500

company, but he can't figure out when a woman is bullshitting him. Or maybe he knows, because he steers me away from her. "There's someone else I want you to meet. This is Christopher."

There have been other boys. Other girls. Most of the time we ignore each other, having bigger problems in our broken rich-kid lives than the stepsibling of the month. Sometimes one of them will take a swipe at me, with sharp words or a surprise shove as we pass in the hallway. A preemptive strike, so I know better than to mess with them.

I don't want to mess with them. They'll be gone by next year.

There's no reason Christopher should be different.

Except that he is.

Even in a burst of sunlight he manages to look like a shadow, with raven hair and onyx eyes. He's taller than me, taller than Daddy. His arms solid and muscled beneath the thin cotton of his black T-shirt. He's wearing jeans, technically, but nothing about him is casual. Not the way he holds himself, as if he needs to guard something— maybe himself. And definitely not the way he's looking at me, intensity a physical brush against my skin, like he's made of ocean and I'm sand, washed away, washed away, becoming smooth and pliable beneath him.

He inclines his head. "Your dad talks a lot about you."

"He never mentioned you," I say before I can stop myself. I would have remembered. *He looks like some kind of conquering warrior, like a knight from the old medieval days. The kind who would have defended the peasants, but who would also have demanded his due.*

Daddy makes a disapproving sound. "Harper."

The corner of Christopher's mouth turns up. "There's not much to say."

"Liar," I say before I can stop myself. "I bet you're top ten percent of your class."

"Graduated valedictorian," Daddy says, pride rich in his voice. "Now he's in his first year at Emerson studying business with a 4.0 GPA. You could learn a thing or two from him."

It's really not surprising Daddy has a new wife every year. The only thing he knows how to do with the female of the species is make us mad. "He can get good grades, but can he paint a three-story Medusa on the wall of the gymnasium?"

A rueful laugh. "That little stunt cost me a brand-new science lab."

Even two coats of thick white primer hadn't completely covered the shape of her thick lips and wild snake hair, painted dark and angry in the small hours of the morning, using the folded-up accordion stands for scaffolding.

The new wife makes some kind of cooing sound, like a bird on the street, and Daddy goes to make her a drink. That leaves me and Christopher standing on the deck, the echo of his perfect GPA and my costly little stunt hanging in the air between us.

"Daddy seems to love you," I say, unable to keep the venom from my voice.

He laughs softly, which infuriates me. "You're one to talk."

"He's *my* dad. Of course he loves me."

"Of course. That's why you need to paint the gym to get him to notice you."

Asshole. "You don't know anything about me."

"So you aren't a poor little rich girl?"

There's a twinge in my chest. "We both know you'll be gone next year. I'll never see you again, and you'll never see me, so let's just stay out of each other's way for the next week, okay?"

"Sure you wouldn't rather learn a thing or two from me?" he asks, mocking.

"If I want to know how to make enemies and alienate people, I'll call you."

He blinks, and I think for a minute that I may have actually struck a nerve. Then his eyes harden. "I'll stay out of your way," he says, his voice so cold it makes me shiver even as the sun beats its heavy blanket on my bare shoulders. It's not the worst encounter I've ever had with a stepsibling, but it's the first time I think I started it. Apparently I'm not above lashing out first, if the boy in question is smart and handsome enough.

Though he isn't really a boy, this one. His first year at Emerson College. Business school. No wonder Daddy loves him. He probably thinks he's found his true heir, because his wild daughter isn't going to take over the family empire. That will never be me, but I was right about one thing. Christopher will be gone next year. They always are.

CHAPTER TWO

Family Money

I MANAGE TO avoid him the rest of the day, napping after brunch and ignoring him at dinner.

Our cabins are on the same floor, below the galley and above the master bedroom where our parents sleep. Thankfully he keeps his word and leaves me alone, even stepping aside to let me pass when I head back to the observation deck at midnight. I suck in a breath to make extra sure no part of my body touches his.

Wind whips at my hair, salty and cool, as I step out of the hold.

I grasp the cold metal railing and let it ground me. Why does Christopher bother me so much? In my pocket there are a couple of joints and a lighter. I light myself something to calm down, because I would rather not know the answer to that question.

In a practiced move I swing my leg over the railing and pull myself up. This is my favorite place to sit, from the time I was six years old and my nanny would fall asleep in the room next door. I can pretend the yacht isn't here, pretend it's just me and the ocean, rocking and rocking. The movement bounces me softly, my ass against the metal bar.

Weed makes it better, more like a meditation. The more drags I take, the more it feels like the whole world is rocking, and maybe I'm the only one sitting still.

"Do you have a death wish?"

The question comes out of the darkness behind me, and I jump, almost slipping off the rail. I manage to catch myself, clutching the metal bar with one hand and the joint with another. Survival and sanity, the two most important things in life. "Do you always hide in the shadows?"

"Whenever possible."

I snort, which is a friendlier sound than I want to make with him. "That doesn't surprise me."

He takes a step forward and holds out his hand. "You're making me nervous."

"That's kind of my standard operating procedure," I say, ignoring his hand and taking another drag. "You get good grades. I get into trouble."

"So the death wish thing…"

"Pretty accurate," I say, wishing he would go belowdecks. And wishing he wouldn't. There's something complicated about him, the way he makes me want opposite things at the same time. "I don't want to die, but I want to live. People call that having a death wish."

With clear reluctance he pulls his hand back and settles his arms on the railing a few feet away from my ass. His eyes are trained on the dark horizon, but I can tell he's still watching me. "This is what living means? Falling into the ocean with no one around to rescue you?"

I point at the choppy water. "The captain dropped anchor before dinner. We aren't even moving. What do you think is going to happen?"

"Head trauma. Hypothermia. Drowning."

"For your information I've been coming up here by myself for a decade. No one ever comes with me. Haven't fallen overboard once."

"Then statistically speaking, you're overdue."

"Wow, you really are my dad's heir." Part of me is glad to have company on one of my nightly reveries. The other part of me feels the distinct intrusion of having a stranger in my space.

"What?"

"Go back down and play with your calculator."

There's a pained pause. "I can't. Not when I know you're up here, getting high and hanging off a two-hundred-foot yacht. If something happened to you—"

"Nothing's going to happen to me." The sea takes that moment to bump bump bump me, my ass a full two inches off the rail with every pull of the yacht. I'm holding on tight so I don't go flying, not forward or backward, my perch secure.

"Are you sure you wouldn't rather paint a mythical creature on the observation deck?"

"I know you're making fun of me right now, but no. I don't have enough paint for that."

"Can you just sit on a deck chair like a normal person?"

"Do I look normal to you? Don't answer that."

There's a flash of white teeth. That's how I know he's smiling even though the rest of his face is in shadow. The smile is there one second and gone the next, as temporary as his presence in my life but strangely momentous. "I'm sorry I called you a poor little rich girl."

"Are you just saying that so I'll get off the railing?"

"Is it working?"

"No, but I appreciate the effort."

And strangely that was true. Not many people have ever cared enough to follow me up to the deck at midnight, to make sure I didn't fall into the ocean. Definitely not one of the stepsiblings, who would probably have given me a little push to get rid of the competition for the inheritance.

It makes me want to prove myself to him, to convince him that I'm worth saving even if he apparently already thinks so. "Medusa wasn't for attention. I mean, she was, but not because I wanted Daddy to pay for a new science lab."

"Then why'd you do it?"

"This girl got roofied at a party."

He sucks in a breath. "Harper."

"It wasn't me." I glance sideways to see his black eyes staring at me, so hard and fierce it almost seems possible that he can go back in time and rip the balls off a frat boy. What would he say if he knew my past? "It wasn't me, I swear. I wasn't even friends with her."

After a searching look, he turns back to the ocean. "A girl got roofied."

"Everyone knew about it, like the next day. One of the football players slipped it in her drink, and then the football team, I mean the *entire* football team, took advantage of her."

"Christ."

"They suspended the guy who brought the roofie to the party, one of the players, but not the one who gave it to her—the quarterback. And not the rest of the team. A big game was coming up. You can't play a game without all your players."

He's quiet a moment. "I'm sorry."

For that I pass him the joint and watch while he takes a drag, his lips touching where mine have been. "The honor society set up a protest and everyone who went got suspended. And after all that there wasn't a single word about the party in the local papers. The morning before the game there was going to be a big pep rally with the cheerleaders and the school's donors. The press was going to be there. They had the janitors stay late shining the floor. Real press, from a newspaper that wouldn't take money not to print the story."

He passes the joint back to me. "So you painted Medusa."

"She was raped by Poseidon, who so happened to be the school mascot." I have to blink away stupid tears. I don't know why it would make me cry now, when it didn't before. Not when I had to walk down the hallway next to boys who would hurt me if they had the chance. When

I had to wear my skirt a certain length and my hair a certain way, as if I was the reason they were cruel.

"Did everyone turn to stone?"

I look down at the water, where I can see more white crests against the ink. It looks rough for a calm night. "The reporter took pictures and started asking questions, but he didn't get the whole story that day. A week later the story was printed. The entire team was suspended. The headmaster was ready to suspend me too, but Daddy flew down and smoothed it over."

"The science lab."

"Which means I'm no better than those players, using my family money."

His voice is soft enough I have to strain to hear it over the murmur of the waves. "You're plenty better, Harper. Don't you ever doubt that. You're fucking gold."

My heart skips a beat. I should know better than to fall for a line, but this boy has me messed up. I'm caught by his eyes, which are somehow darker than the sea beneath us and infinitely more deep. I'm drowning there; that must be the reason I don't feel it coming.

Lurch.

Dip.

My hand finds cold metal, and I have a moment of sweet relief—until the slickness of sea spray coats my palm and I lose my grip. For a moment I'm suspended in air, my gaze still locked on his, my shock reflected in that black mirror.

And then I'm falling.

CHAPTER THREE

Deadweight

MY PARENTS BOTH tell the story of when I was two years old. One minute I was standing on the deck. The next I had fallen into the Massachusetts Bay. They both had a heart attack, or so the story goes, until they ran to the edge and saw me swimming around like a fish, more comfortable in water than on land.

I'm not sure whether I really learned to swim quite that naturally or why I was left to toddle around the docks without someone holding my hand, but I do love to swim. I've even jumped off the deck of the yacht into the water, too impatient to climb down the long swim steps.

I'm falling backward and twisted, unable to see how far I'm falling. Unable to see anything—but I can feel it, the slam of the surface at my back, the shock of freezing cold. And then it surrounds me, heavy weight dragging me down. The air leaves me in a rush; by the time I can take another breath, I'm fully submerged.

It's pitch-black, impossible to know which way is up. Any direction I go could be taking me deeper. My throat burns with salt. Panic threatens to overwhelm me. My whole body clenches, fighting the instinct to breathe in deep and fill my lungs with water.

Something touches my side, and I squirm away in terror. Even stoned and in shock I remember there might be sharks. What if they heard me splashing? What if they sense my fear?

Except there's a grip on my arm—a hand, not teeth. It drags me up in a whoosh of water, and we break the surface together.

The cold night air has never felt so good in my lungs. I gasp and gasp, unwilling to stop breathing after even a few seconds without it, unable to calm down.

Something is shoved under my arms. The white and red of a life preserver. Christopher must have thrown one down before he jumped in after me. In a kaleidoscope of stars the world comes into focus. The water, lapping at me like a living thing. Christopher, his dark hair wet, his grip on my wrist firm as he tows us toward the yacht. And the boat itself, waves drawing intermittent shadows across the white bow.

It might have been ten years before we reach

the bottom of the swim steps. Or maybe only ten minutes. I'm deadweight on the life preserver, unable to kick even once to help make progress.

"Can you climb?" Christopher shouts.

I stare at him, unable to process the words. The cold has done something to my body, made me sluggish and stiff. It's done the same thing to my brain.

"Let's get you through the middle," he says, reaching for the life ring. "I'll make sure you're secure and then go for help."

Sudden panic is enough to jolt me out of my shock. "No."

"It will only take a minute."

He thinks I'm worried about being left alone in the water. More than that I'm worried about the disappointment on Daddy's face. "I can climb," I say, my voice shaky and thin.

Christopher stares at me for a moment, and when he speaks, his voice is softer. "He won't be mad at you. You should hear the way he talks about you when you're not there."

That's exactly why I can't let him know I was smoking a joint and falling overboard. He wants me to be like Christopher—to be the valedictorian and go to business school. That's something I'll never be able to do for him, but at least I can spare him this. "Please."

"Fuck," he mutters.

In that moment I realize he already knows this will be a secret. Our secret. Because he didn't follow procedure. He should have shouted for help and hit the emergency button first. And he definitely shouldn't have jumped in after me, not without someone else on deck to pull us both back up. An unbroken sky rises from the metal railing above us. The night is quiet except for our fast breathing and the lap of the water. "Thank you," I whisper.

"I swear to God," he says darkly, "if you fall and die, I'll kill you myself."

That would make me laugh if I were capable of doing anything other than pant. He makes me go first, though I'm not sure how he would manage to catch me if I fell. If there's one thing I know by now, it's that he would try. So I focus on each rung with every ounce of determination in me, grip the textured metal and pray there's enough muscle left inside me to hold on. There are a thousand steps up the side of the yacht. A million of them. It's my own personal journey to the promised land, and it tests my determination with every aching pull.

When I reach the top, I push myself through

the railing and collapse onto the deck.

A warm body tumbles beside me, but I can't look sideways. There's only the stars, unblinking. Then a face appears above me. Christopher, looking wet and strong and grim. "We should go back to shore. The fall. The cold. You should have a doctor look at you."

"N-n-no."

"Harper. You're freezing."

There's no way to argue that point, not when I'm shaking so hard my teeth are chattering. I think that's a good sign. I read that somewhere. It means the body is warm enough to shiver, but I can't get the words out through the violent movement.

He curses again and disappears from my view. I close my eyes in quiet despair. He's gone to get Daddy, and there's nothing I can do to stop him. The week we would have spent at sea, now we'll spend it in some fancy emergency room even though I'm fine.

Not enough time has passed when hands force their way under me. Then I'm lifted, tucked close to a body as wet as mine but so much warmer. Christopher carries me belowdecks, turning carefully to the side so I don't bump against the narrow walls.

He lays me down on my bed, and my arms are made of lead. My legs might as well be anvils, that's how useful they would be if I were in the water right now. I'm helpless in front of this person who should be my enemy. *Poor little rich girl,* he called me, and I want to cry and rage because he's right about me.

His hands move to the button of my jeans, and I suck in a breath. My mind was on sharks and freezing water, but now I'm thinking about roofies. I'm thinking about a girl who can't protect herself. About Poseidon and Medusa.

"Christopher," I whisper, though I'm not sure what I'm asking.

He glares at me, his eyes black with a strange heat. "You have two options. Either I call your dad here or I make sure you're warm. You pick."

You pick. In those two words he restores my faith in him—strange, because I wouldn't have said I had faith at all. I know I need to get out of my wet clothes, and my body is too hurt by the freezing cold to be useful. "Don't look."

After a beat he nods, facing away from me. Then he turns off the dim bedside lamp, bathing us only in moonlight from the port window. He undresses me with clumsy efficiency, his fingers clearly numb and struggling against the waterlogged fabric. I feel somehow colder by the time he's done, the damp clothes in a heap on the floor, my naked skin exposed to the room.

And then I watch while he undresses himself, faster and rougher with his body than he was with mine. His clothes land on top of mine, and then he pulls us both under the covers.

He's naked. The thought is enough to make me blush, even when there shouldn't be any energy in my body for such an act. But he holds me close, tight enough I can't make out where his male parts meet my female parts. There are only two bodies here, clinging together for warmth, creating a little cocoon. Exhaustion makes my eyelids heavy.

"One of my mom's husbands got into bed with me once."

Every part of his body becomes stiff. "What the fuck?"

"It was bad. Not like this. This is nice."

"I swear to God, Harper."

"It's okay," I say, the words slurred together. "I told Mom the next day and we moved out of his mansion, even though it was really nice. He owned this big job website. Don't tell Daddy. He would freak out even though it was a long time ago."

He holds me tighter, his face pressed to my hair. "I'm not going to touch you. I'm only staying here until you don't feel like an ice cube, and then I'm moving to the chair."

"Thanks," I say, the word coming out long and slow.

He sighs. "Go to sleep, Harper. And for the love of God, don't die."

A death wish, he'd called it. "Want to live," I mumble before the dreams take me down. It's only later that I think that everything changed that night. Not because I fell into the bay or because he pulled me out. Because I confessed that in my sleepy-shocked state. It set us on the course to ruin, what made him the white knight to my damsel in distress.

CHAPTER FOUR

Temporary

I WAKE UP gasping for air, a nightmare of being submerged in water pressing against my consciousness. My muscles ache as I stretch in the bunk, looking up at familiar knots in the ceiling. What the hell did I dream about? There's grit in my eyes as if I spent all evening at a bonfire, drinking cheap beer from a plastic cup and ignoring the frat boys on the beach.

My mind moves slow and careful. I'm not sure I want the memory that happens next, but it comes anyway. Not a nightmare. Not a dream. I fell overboard last night.

And Christopher Bardot saved me.

That would be shocking, but not as shocking as the memory of him naked in the moonlight, climbing into bed, his warm skin flush against mine. He's gone now, enough that I would think it really could have been a dream. Except for the faint scent of him that remains, something woodsy and male that managed to survive a dip in the Atlantic.

My phone rings from the nightstand, my mother's picture flashing on the screen. It's a photo I took when she was laughing at the beach and didn't think I was watching her. Completely different than the beauty queen smile she uses when looking at a camera. There's a bittersweet sensation whenever I think about her when I'm with Daddy, a feeling of betrayal I can't shake for loving him even though he hates her so much.

"Hey, Mom."

"You didn't call to say you got there safely," she says, a small pout in her voice.

"Shit. I'm sorry. I should have texted at least."

"That's okay. I'm sure you're busy there."

That's my opening to tell her about Daddy's new wife. She used to scoop every detail out of me like I was a melon, hollowed out and left dry. "Mostly I've been sleeping."

"Are you still in bed?" she asks, laughing a little. "Me too."

That makes me smile. "You should be relaxing. You're a free woman. Stay out late. Go to a party. You don't have a kid at home to take care of."

"I don't think I've had to take care of you since you were eight."

That's probably true. I was the one who brought her breakfast and her medicine in the morning. I signed my own permission slips and called the driver when my art club meeting ended.

"How is he?" she asks, her voice soft and a little sad.

"He's good. Same old Daddy."

"And his... family?"

"I'm not sure. His new wife seems okay. She mostly just ignores me, which is fine. She has a son, though. He's... older."

She must sense something in my words, because her tone changes. "How much older? He isn't being a bully, is he? Or worse?"

"It's nothing like that," I promise her, because I wouldn't put it past her to fly out to Logan International by tonight if I didn't reassure her.

She felt terrible about the job-website man. He'd needed to get drunk to come into my bedroom, which means his reflexes were slow. I ran out and woke up Mom, who had us out of the mansion and in a motel room by morning.

"Christopher's nice, actually. Nicer than I expected."

A pause. "Don't get too close, Harper. It's only temporary."

I can't blame her for the warning. She knows

all too well how temporary being the wife of Graham St. Claire can be. Theirs had been a whirlwind relationship, the kind that every man and woman envied. By all accounts, even their own, they had been in love.

And then something had happened. To this day I still don't know what.

Now they hate each other. It scares me when I think about it, how two people can go from love to hate so quickly. It scares me enough that I try *not* to think about it. About the way Daddy could have given her enough money to be set for life, it would have been pennies to him, but he denied her everything that wasn't court-ordered out of spite. The child support they negotiated was contingent on a third party auditing her bank account to make sure every cent of it goes to my care. If she eats a Snickers bar purchased from his check, he could sue.

If that's what happens to people in love, I don't want any part of it.

I find Daddy at the breakfast table, the newspaper propped open like I knew it would be. He's not content without reading three newspapers every morning, even when we're on a trip. It comes ferried to us via a speedboat at five a.m., along with fresh supplies because God knows what we would do without catch-of-the-day lobster for dinner every night.

"Morning," he says without looking up.

I dig in the pile for the Art & Style section, like I always do. Other kids may have read Garfield, but I've always been a museum opening kind of girl. "Good morning."

A chocolate chip pancake appears in front of me, the butter melting in a delicious puddle. I'm a continent away from our apartment in LA, but it might as well be a different planet. I don't have to use my lunch money to tip the bellman so word doesn't get back that we're flat broke. Don't have to work an evening shift at the deli down the block to pay the bills.

"How's your mother?" The question comes in that neutral voice, so without inflection that it conveys everything. The way they end up screaming at each other on the phone. The very careful way that Daddy agrees to pay for my prep school tuition and room-and-board fees in a private suite—but nothing else. On that point he stands firm.

I once told my friend in middle school, because she didn't understand how the daughter of a billionaire couldn't afford to take the school trip to France. *I would be pissed,* she said, sounding scandalized. *Like he's trying to control you with money, even though he has so much.* It doesn't make me angry, because I know he has terrible and complicated feelings about money.

Terrible and complicated feelings about money, like my mother.

It's something we pass down through generations, like a grandfather clock that chimes every time your bank account rises or falls. A legacy and a family curse. I'm not naive enough to think I'll manage to escape that.

"Good," I say, because we decided a long time ago, when I was only ten, that it was me and her against the world. If I tell Daddy what it's like when she's between husbands, how it feels to be hungry or cold, he'll take me away from her.

"And how's school?"

"I'm working on a sculpture for the spring art festival. My teacher said it's inspired and strange and sinister. That's a direct quote."

Daddy gives me a fond look, mixed with the kind of bemusement he's always given me. It would be so much easier if I loved the stock market or international law. "Christopher told me about last night."

Panic squeezes my throat. That bastard.

Maybe it's not fair to get mad at someone

who saved my life, but still. He seemed like he was going to be cool about it. I'm two seconds away from saying, *He took a drag of the weed too!* Before reason prevails. Never give them eight words when two will suffice.

"He did?"

"I had half a mind to wake you up, make sure you get on the East Coast schedule right away. Christopher told me he heard you playing music until late, so we decided to let you sleep in."

For a second I'm struck by the horror of Daddy walking in on me and Christopher, both naked and tangled beneath the sheets. That's only superseded by the horror of him knowing that I fell overboard last night. Thank God someone woke up early—and that someone appears at the table, looking annoyingly well rested compared to the bags that must be under my eyes.

"Are you a vampire?" I demand as he pours himself a cup of coffee.

"Don't mind her," Daddy warns in a tone that says teenage girls are stupid. I'm hardly the person to disprove that, but it has way more to do with changing prep schools every single year than the fact that I have a vagina. It's easier to let everyone think I don't care.

"I have been known to order my steak rare,"

Christopher offers.

I nod in satisfaction. "You have that whole old-soul thing going on. No wonder you're getting straight A's. You probably wrote the textbook when you were a professor. And now you have to get a new degree as someone else or people will get suspicious."

"The typo on page seventy-eight haunts me to this day," he says in a grave voice.

Daddy stares at me like I'm speaking a different language. "I don't suppose it factors into this conversation that vampires aren't real?"

"Not with that attitude, they aren't."

A slow smile spreads on Christopher's face, and my breath stutters. It's the kind of smile so rare and precious it could be sold at Sotheby's. *Quality,* the auctioneer would say, standing in front of the well-dressed crowd, *in its raw, natural state.* The world is going to want that smile. It's going to polish him into a sharp geometric shape, hard and gleaming. And it will be worth more money than God.

CHAPTER FIVE

The Best Curtsy

I T'S NOT UNTIL that night that I find Christopher alone, head bent over a thick textbook at his desk, the lamp casting shadows on his furrowed brow. It softens me more than it should, seeing him working hard when no one's watching. "This a bad time?" I ask, leaning against the doorframe.

He turns to face me, his expression inscrutable. "Would it stop you if I said yes?"

I pretend to consider this. "You *did* save my life, but I think that only means I have to save your life back. Or maybe give you my firstborn child? They skipped this part in my etiquette class, but I'm pretty sure I don't have to respect your time either way."

"You took an etiquette class?"

"Standard operating procedure for any debutante."

He shakes his head as if bewildered. "I shouldn't be surprised."

"My curtsy is literally the best curtsy, thank you very much."

"Not that you're a debutante. Just—" He waves a hand at the cabin, the whole yacht. "This whole thing. It's kind of insane, if you don't mind me saying so."

That draws me farther into the room. I perch on the end of his bed, which is still neatly made after turndown service. "You didn't grow up with the silver-spoon thing?"

He snorts. "The only thing silver we had was a ten-year-old Toyota Camry."

"Then how did your mom bag my dad?" I say the question without thinking. There are too many wives in too many years for me to treat the marriages as anything sacred. Or love, for that matter. Daddy doesn't even bother inviting me to the ceremony, though I never really know if that says more about the women or about me.

Christopher shrugs like he doesn't take offense. "Mom came from money, but when she married my dad, they cut her off. He was a hard worker. A regular office job. A 401K. That kind of thing. Then he got cancer, and I... I don't really begrudge her this. It's what she wants."

"That's very understanding of you."

"It's not exactly a hardship," he says. "Even if

I do have to dive into cold water."

"Thank you," I say softly, meaning it more than words can convey. It's a situation plenty of boys would have taken advantage of. The kind of boys who bring roofies to parties and get away with things because they can. The only kind of boys I've known until now.

He shakes his head, pushing aside my gratitude. "You wouldn't have died. Probably."

"I'm glad you're good at the whole numbers business thing, because a career in motivational speaking is out of the question for you."

He leans forward and opens his mouth, as if he's going to say something important. And then he stops. When he finally speaks, it's something I never would have expected. "You're smart," he says, and I laugh.

"What?"

"You're smart, but you don't want anyone to know."

"I'm *not* smart, as my grades can definitely attest. We can't all be valedictorian, can we?"

He laughs a little. "You are so full of shit."

"Excuse me? My report cards are very clear on this issue. I am the absolute best at failing. If there were grades given for failing, I would get straight A's."

When I was in third grade, the teacher called my mother in for a conference and showed her my math workbook. I had used the numbers like an abstract paint-by-numbers, turning the pages into stained-glass drawings of flowers and puppies and this one grim reaper with its scythe made out of a column of fractions. It's not that I can't add or subtract or even do advanced derivatives. It's that my mind will flit away like a butterfly in a meadow filled with flowers.

"Okay," Christopher says. "But I know the truth."

Frustration makes me huff, which is a lot safer than letting myself smile at him. "Fine, but I know the truth about you."

One dark eyebrow rises. "What's that?"

The insight hits me with the same clarity as I saw every page in that workbook, the possibility rising up out of the framework. "This whole thing. The insanity of the yacht and the silver spoon, you want it so bad it hurts. That's why you study so hard. Because you want this life as bad as your mom, but you're working for it in a different way."

The silence descends on us, as heavy and cold as the water. His throat works. "That obvious, huh?"

My brain, usually good at comebacks, falls suddenly silent. There are things I could say to ease the moment: *I didn't mean it, I'm sure it's not true.* But those would be lies. We're sitting in the cabin with only nakedness between us, the same way we were last night. "It doesn't mean anything bad about you." At least that much is true.

He laughs without humor. "It doesn't mean I'm a greedy asshole?"

"Oh, for sure, you're definitely a greedy asshole. Who isn't? Everyone wants money. Very few are willing to work as hard as you to earn it."

"Listen," he says, seeming uncertain for once. "What you said about that guy. The one who owned the job website. The one who—"

"I shouldn't have told you that," I say, my cheeks burning like fire. "It was a moment of weakness. Which I seem to be having around you with unfortunate frequency."

"Maybe we should tell your dad. He could make sure that—"

"Absolutely not. No offense, but you've been my stepbrother for like a month. You don't know the history in my family. That guy is gone, and the best thing to do is leave it alone."

My parents alternately hate each other and love each other, but that isn't what breaks us. It's the money that fractures us into a million sharp pieces.

Like the men in my life, money is only temporary.

And if I never want either of them, I won't be disappointed when they're gone.

38

CHAPTER SIX

Admissions Essay

Dear Christopher,

My mother married a German count, which is exactly as pretentious as it sounds. We're moving to Frankfurt and that means a boarding school with new rules and lesson plans where I'm already going to be behind. I hope you don't mind that I'm writing you, because I know we're not technically related anymore.

PS. Who's going to dive in and rescue me on spring break?

Dear Harper,

Thank you for writing to me, even if we aren't related anymore. If it's any consolation, you feel as much a sister to me as you did before. Which is to say, not much. I'm sorry to hear about the new boarding school. I hope they have lots of paint.

PS. Don't sit on the rail at midnight, and whatever you do, don't die.

Dear Christopher,

Germany is cold and guess what? They speak German. It's hard to make friends when the only things I know how to say are "Yes, ma'am" and "Which way is the bathroom?" I'm super popular.

You will be pleased to know that while I did smoke a joint on the railing, I had my phone in my pocket in a waterproof case. So even if I had fallen in, which I didn't, I could have called the yacht's concierge line and gotten rescued. Three cheers for technology.

PS. My new stepbrother wears twenty pounds of cologne and has a goatee.

Dear Harper,

It's kind of strange how different the second year is from the first. In the freshman classes they kept talking about weeding people out (which doesn't mean what you think it does) and how hard it would be, but I felt like I had a handle on things. Now they're acting like it's straightforward and I'm staying up late every night banging my head against these textbooks.

I feel like I'm drowning here.

PS. If I had written this textbook, I deserve to be shot. With a silver bullet.

Dear Christopher,

You have an amazing brain, which is something I can state without any hesitation because you said I was smart—so obviously you have a clear and accurate understanding of the world. Plus, Daddy keeps talking about how you're going to do great things.

And I'm not just saying that because

you're a vampire who wrote a shitty text-book.

PS. For the love of God, don't die.

Dear Harper,

Finals damn near killed me, but I kept your letter on my desk. I figured as long as you had ordered me not to die, I had no choice but to listen. That's how saving your life works, right? I never took eti-quette class, so I'm just guessing here.

Your dad gave a speech at commencement and took me out to dinner. He said you were doing some kind of big art exhibit in New York City. That's incredible.

PS. Why didn't you tell me about it?

Dear Christopher,

That's exactly how saving my life works, and congratulations on graduating!!! The only reason I applied to Smith College is my art professor. Her work is amazing. In my admissions essay I wrote about the Medusa painting. I thought they only made interns read those things, but Professor Mills found out and asked me to do an exhibit.

I thought about vandalizing the school and tearing out the wall of the gym, but shipping rates are ridiculous. So instead I'm doing a series of canvas paintings about the myth.

PS. I'm enclosing an invitation to the exhibit in case you can make it.

CHAPTER SEVEN

Breaking and Entering

I
T SEEMED IMPOSSIBLE that Christopher would spend his weekend traveling to New York City for a girl he knew for a week a couple years ago. The fact that we kept in touch felt surreal, almost a dream, like the night I fell into the bay. That we were stepsiblings, if only for a few months, made it more strange, not less. I couldn't be sure what I wanted from him, not even in the privacy of my mind. What were the odds a man like him would be interested in a girl like me?

I never told Daddy that Christopher and I wrote letters. At first I wasn't sure what he would think about it. And then it became weird to mention, as if I'd been keeping a secret. That's what the letters were—a secret. An escape.

A lifeline, like the red and white round buoy.

The exhibit becomes bigger than I thought it would, once my mom finds out about it. She invites every friend and enemy she ever knew in New York City, and the whole thing blows up. It would have been nice to have a small show filled mostly with the art scene, people who would appreciate the work more than the champagne.

But I accepted my mother's ambitions in society a long time ago. As Christopher said once, *It's not exactly a hardship. Even if I do have to dive into cold water.*

All the pieces for the show are packed into foam-padded crates stacked along the foyer of the penthouse suite. Daddy's paying the bill, of course. Mom's last divorce gave her the smallest payout yet, which had less to do with a prenup and more to do with the man's failure in the stock market. Only the main piece remains propped against the window, surrounded by tubes of paint and a disarray of brushes. I can't seem to stop myself from dabbling at it, even though I've lost any perspective on whether I'm making it better or worse.

Mom breezes from her bedroom in a casual blouse of ivory silk and skinny jeans, the perpetual cloud of Chanel achingly familiar. "Oh, baby, are you still working on it? It's perfect, you know."

I twirl a dry paintbrush in my fingers. "This is the one they'll write about."

She comes and gives me a kiss on the forehead. "I'm so proud of you. Everyone is going to be blown away by your talent."

Despite our weird money issues, I love my parents. Mom always supports me, and even if she can't settle down to save her life, that only makes her human. Daddy is puzzled by everything I do, but he's coming to the exhibit. Cancelled a business trip to Japan to be here.

The fact that they'll be in the same room for two hours is cause for concern, but at least neither of them are married to someone else right now. That makes it ten percent less likely to devolve into a screaming match by the end.

I sigh, flopping back onto the oversize leather couch. "Don't worry about me. I just need to stare at this for approximately twenty-four more hours, and then I never have to see it again."

Mom checks her lipstick in a gold-leaf mirror. It's already perfect, of course. "Are you sure? I can stay in tonight. Sandra and the girls will understand."

"No, you should definitely go out. We haven't been in NYC in forever." It was back to LA after the relationship with the German count ended, and thank God for small favors.

She smiles. "You're the best daughter."

"I really am." I blow her a kiss. "Now go have fun. That's an order."

After putting a few smudges of Atomic Red on my cheeks, she floats out the door. It will be good for her to meet her girlfriends, even if they are a pack of conniving hyenas. She hasn't been this excited since before Robert the day trader asked her to marry him.

And besides, it wouldn't help for her to hover over me. I really am going to drive myself crazy in the final hours leading up to the exhibit. This piece will get auctioned off at the end of the night, and the money will go to a charity to help victims of rape and abuse. There's every chance that Daddy will be the highest bidder, not because he likes the painting but because money is the only way he knows how to show his support of my weird interests. Even knowing that, I can't help but obsess over this piece.

The other pieces show Medusa in various stages of her life; with her three Gorgon sisters, beautiful and pristine, being held down by Poseidon, being cursed by Athena for the "crime" of being raped in her temple, her hair turned to snakes, her face turning every man to stone. You would think that's enough tragedy for the Greeks, but then they had to behead her.

The other pieces tell the story of her life and death, but the centerpiece of the show is a simple portrait like the one that appeared on the wall of the gymnasium, sprung from my rage and fear and helplessness, the look in her eyes mirrored in every girl who walked the hallways with me.

I had only a few hours between when the custodians went home and when school staff arrived in the morning, which meant I had to work fast—and that was good; the time limit gave me the intensity I needed to complete the piece. The painting in front of me is good. Maybe even my best work, but there's something missing. A sense of necessity. That I would have painted the wall of that gymnasium or died trying.

Maybe it's impossible for something created to exhibit to match that intensity.

Or maybe I've just failed at art in a spectacularly public fashion.

My phone vibrates with a text from across the room. It's probably Avery, my best friend from Smith College, who's staying at a hotel in Times Square. If she offers to get drunk with me, that's how I'll be spending tonight, I already know.

It's Christopher.

Two words and suddenly I can't breathe. Is he texting me to wish me good luck the night before my big show? Does he even remember that it's tomorrow? Or is this some random Christopher in a city that must have thousands of them, who somehow got my number and is now going to send me an unsolicited dick pic?

My hands are shaking, which I prefer to attribute to nerves about the upcoming show than about the fact that Christopher is texting me for the first time. *Heyyyy, stranger.*

There's a full two minutes, during which my heart beats approximately twelve thousand times and I think of ten terrifying ways he might have been injured after texting me.

I'm at the airport about to get in a cab. Do you have plans for dinner or are you going to an uber hip artist spot where they drink kombucha and complain about capitalism?

A smile spreads over my face before I can stop it. He's here in New York City. For me. And he's possibly inviting me to dinner? The suite suddenly becomes a fun-house mirror, everything in all different shapes, leaving me dizzy and out of breath.

Actually I'm in my hotel room, thinking about slashing this painting, but they only sent up a butter knife with room service. After a moment I send another text, *You can come hang out if you want. There's no kombucha but we can raid the minibar.*

No vandalism until I get there.

I might have a sensitive artist's soul, but I'm still a girl.

A girl with an unfortunate, painful, and totally inappropriate crush.

Which means I spring up and raid my closet for something other than a paint-splattered tank top and ripped shorts. I pull a brush through my hair, which is about all I can do before falling back on my bed, wondering why I want to impress someone I barely know. It's not like I've never been on a date before. I've been on lots of dates, with frat boys who think I'm going to fawn over them for knowing how to kick a ball or making a reference to Kant. Whatever.

I don't think Christopher has ever tried to impress me. I also don't think he wants to get me into bed. At least, he had me naked once and didn't try anything. So where does that leave us? I'm not fifteen anymore, if that had ever been what kept him away from me. I'm eighteen now, and ironically more fully aware of my cluelessness as a sexual being than I was back then.

It's another hour until he knocks on the door.

And I definitely don't run to the door or stand in front of it for two whole minutes, trying to catch my breath and pretend like I haven't been waiting for him since he sent that text. Since before that, if I'm totally honest. Since I sent the invitation, pretending I didn't care if he ignored it.

Since he dived in after me through the water, the first person to meet me where I was instead of where they wanted me to be.

When I open the door, he looks rumpled and travel-worn and so handsome after being on a plane that it's indecent. "Hey, stranger," he says softly, his eyes a sleek ocean surface at night. It's been three years since I've seen him, and he looks harder and softer at the same time.

There are lots of ways I can say hello to him that will make me seem mature. Instead I throw my arms around his broad shoulders and press my face into his neck, breathing him in. "It's the worst thing I've ever made, and everyone's going to look at it, and I want to die."

He stands stock-still for a moment, as if too surprised to even move. Then his arms wrap around me. He holds me like the whole world could batter us from every side and we would still be safe clinging together like this. He holds me like I'm running out of air and he knows the way to the surface. "It will be okay, Harper. I promise you."

There are embarrassing tears on my lashes

when I pull back. "This would be less humiliating if I were throwing an artistic tantrum and throwing things. Crying is so pedestrian."

"I'm sure that vase would make a satisfying crash," he offers gently.

The weird thing is I know he would let me throw it, if that's what I needed. Or cry on his shoulder if that's what I need instead. "Come inside," I say, dragging him by the hand so he has to scramble to grab the handle of his carry-on before the heavy hotel door slams behind him.

I need a minute to compose myself, so I drop his hand and head for the minibar. There are tiny bottles of wine and rum and vodka. "Do you know how to make drinks?" I ask over the *clink* of little glass containers. "The only things I know how to make have the ingredients in the name, like rum and Coke or a whiskey sour."

"Sour isn't an ingredient," he says, sounding distracted.

"Of course it is," I say, glancing back at him. And then freezing when I see he's standing directly in front of Medusa, staring at her like she has the secrets of the universe in her eyes. "Oh."

"Goddamn, Harper. This is... there aren't words."

My throat suddenly feels dry, and I have to

force myself to swallow. I feel strangely buoyant as I stand and cross the few yards between us. "Disappointing? You can tell me."

He looks at me like I'm insane. "This is incredible. There's so much talent, but it's the way it makes you feel her rage and her vulnerability that's incredible. It belongs in the museums next to O'Keeffe and Kahlo, and even then people would stop and stare at this."

"I didn't know you knew about art," I say lamely.

He shrugs, looking embarrassed. "I don't, but I spent my free credits taking Ancient Greek Symbolism and History of Portraiture and the Female Gaze after you told me about Medusa."

My mouth must be hanging open in a way that's decidedly unladylike, but he couldn't have surprised me more if he said he was going to give away all his worldly possessions and become a monk. "You did?"

"I'm a long way from an expert, but in my amateur and totally biased opinion, this painting is amazing. You have nothing to worry about."

"Okay."

Dark eyes narrow. "You aren't convinced."

"It's not a bad painting, I'm not saying that. It's just not *the* painting. The one I need to show considering I'm only doing this exhibit because of the one I painted on the gym wall."

"Is there a photograph we could enlarge?"

I make a face. "No, that's not the right way. I just need to show them…"

"Spontaneity?"

"Rage."

That slow smile again, the one I still remember clearly in my mind all these years later. It's even more poignant now, knowing that he cares about me enough to take those classes. To visit me on my exhibit when he must have a million things more important to do. "Then let's show them rage. Should we slash everyone's tires while they're looking at the exhibit?"

"I like your dedication, but parking in New York City is a logistical nightmare already without adding in guerilla artistry to the mix."

"Fair," he says. "So what do you have in mind?"

"I want to paint something new for them. Something… real."

"Like while they watch? Performance art?"

The idea dawns on me with a lurch and roll, the way the yacht moved beneath me. And then I'm falling with nothing to catch me. Only someone's here to follow me down. "What if we went to the studio right now?"

He looks exactly the right amount of scandal- ized. And being the pragmatist, he glances at his watch. "It's midnight. How long do we have before they open?"

"Long enough."

For a moment he studies me, and I think he's wondering whether he's going to go along with this crazy plan. Wondering more than me, anyway. If there's one thing this man understands, it's raw determination. He'll be in it with me.

A brief nod. "Breaking and entering it is."

That's how we end up spending all night in a fancy SoHo art studio, its walls bare and white and waiting for the paintings that are stacked in my penthouse suite. That's how I end up painting a Medusa in swirls of purple and teal and pink using a wooden folding chair as my step stool.

I don't know where they planned to put the centerpiece of the show. Probably somewhere front and center, where everyone would see it first. This one's in the back of the studio. You have to look at every other painting first and turn the corner. And then she blazes at you in all her snake-fueled glory. She turns the viewer to stone, if Christopher's look of awe is any indication.

He turns to me, and I'm in awe of this, of

him, of his bleary eyes and the smudges of paint from helping me. Of the expression of pride on his handsome face. How did we get here?

"I don't want to go," I tell him.

"We'll be back in a few hours. But I'm pretty sure I should shower before then." He touches his thumb to my cheek, and it comes away teal. "Probably you too."

"Should we leave them a note or something?"

He hands me one of the paintbrushes, this one tinged with dark purple at the tip. "Sign it. That's enough of a note."

I didn't sign the one I painted in the gym, but I take the paintbrush and swirl my name into the bottom right of the painting, where one of the fierce snakes writhes. "How's that?"

"Perfect," he says, his gaze locked on mine.

My breath catches. "Thank you for helping me."

"No, thank you for letting me be part of this. I went to college with legends in the business world, and I've still never seen anything close to this."

"Careful, or I'll start to think you're complaining about capitalism."

He gives me the slow smile. "Never."

It's devastating, that smile and that ambition.

Devastating the way I can't seem to look away from him, not even when he touches my cheek again. This time he isn't wiping away paint. He cups my face and holds me still. His head lowers in slow degrees, giving me time to stop him.

My body is incapable of moving right now. Even my lungs are frozen, my throat locked tight. Only my heart beats hard enough to hear. It pulses in my lips, waiting, waiting for him.

I spent a good part of the past four hours painting lips that are the focal point of this piece—lips that are full of feminine beauty and eternal regret, of desire and revenge. I've worked through the meaning of every rise, every indent, translated the shadows, but now that I look at Christopher's lips, with their masculine utility, I don't know what any of it means. There's a secret code written all over his skin, the message plain if only I could read it.

His mouth meets mine, and for a moment the warmth stuns me. I can only stand there under the gentle press of him, feeling the heat spread through my face and down my neck. Down my stomach and into my legs.

He touches his tongue against the seam of my lips—a question. And I open my mouth in answer, letting him sweep inside with sleep-drunk desire. We shouldn't be doing this. There are so many reasons why this is wrong, but his hands on my waist feel impossibly right.

A sound comes from me, a moan that would embarrass me if I were thinking. I'm only feeling. Only falling and letting him catch me, as if we're meant to do that forever.

His tongue slides against mine, and it's so intimate I have to gasp. The rush of cool air in my mouth, when he had been so hot, wakes me from the strange slumber. I look into eyes dark and heavy-lidded and more shocked than my own.

He takes a step back, letting his hands fall away. "Shit," he says softly.

I haven't kissed very many boys in my life, not enough to hear all the things they might say after they do it, but this response seems particularly disheartening. As does the way he can't seem to look me in the eyes. "Shit?"

His throat works. "I shouldn't have done that."

Why not? That's what I want to ask. Something to soothe this tangle of hurt and hunger inside me. Instead I say, "Is this because Medusa's watching? She's actually not as innocent as she looks."

He shakes his head. "Don't."

My laugh sounds a little maniacal. "It's kind of weird that she looks innocent at all, right? That's not what people usually say, like, 'oh, she has that girl-next-door look with the snake hair.' But there's definitely something innocent about her."

"Harper."

"She's not shocked because you kissed her."

"You," he says gently. "I kissed *you*."

"And then you said *shit*, which I feel like I should tell you, in case you didn't already know, is not the best thing for a girl's self-esteem, mythical creature or otherwise."

"I'm not sorry I kissed you."

"Then why did you stop?"

"Because you're high on adrenaline right now. And paint fumes."

"You're doing the whole white-knight thing again, aren't you? Only this time you're saving me from you. Boys who think they know better than me are very annoying."

"I don't think if I had kissed you when you opened the hotel room door, you would have been nearly as receptive. Tell me that isn't true, and I'll kiss you until we both run out of breath."

I consider lying, because I want to know what happens when we're both out of breath. But I'm a terrible liar, which is how I got caught for doing the painting in the gym even though I hadn't signed my name. Besides, he's right about one thing—I wouldn't have let him kiss me if I hadn't been delirious from lack of sleep. Does that make the kiss more real or less?

In the end he leaves me on the sidewalk in New York City, a heavy-lidded bellhop standing with the door open, steam rising from grates in the flush of an industrial dawn.

CHAPTER EIGHT

Incomparable

THE STUDIO LOSES their minds, chastising me over e-mail and talking about procedures way more than any place with the words "creative genius" in their Facebook bio should. Thankfully I sleep through most of that, and by the time I wake up at three p.m., Professor Mills has smoothed things over.

I'm wearing a forest velvet Givenchy dress with a wrapped bodice. The head curator seems a little drunk by the time Mom and I show up. "I should have had more faith in you," the curator tells me, eyes bright with excitement and secret champagne. "The phone has been off the hook. Everyone wants a ticket, but we're sold out."

I give her a hug mostly because it looks like she needs one. "Thank you so much for giving me the chance to be here. I'm sorry if I stressed you out, but I just wanted to do a good job."

She bursts into tears and ends up crying into my velvet-clad shoulder about how shitty the New

York art scene is and how this might actually save her. Mostly I get through that encounter by telling myself that it's not really happening, that I fell asleep slumped against Medusa last night and now I'm still sleeping under Christopher's watch.

Professional art movers have already brought over the other pieces, which are being carefully hung beneath heavy spotlights. Caterers are setting up a table of hors d'oeuvre with cheese and olives and sesame-seed-covered pita chips to dip into truffle hummus.

Daddy shows up a half hour before the doors will open and squeezes me tight. "I'm so proud of you, Harper. And so glad I got to see this."

The words strike me as odd, and I squeeze him back. "I'm sorry you had to cancel Japan… but also not sorry. It's no 4.0, but it's all I've got."

"I don't care about your GPA."

That makes me roll my eyes. "Sure you don't."

He cups my face in his hands. "I'm serious. The world is a crazy place, but you already know that. That's why you painted that gymnasium in the first place. I just want you to be safe and secure, and if that means making grades and doing what society expects, that's the only reason I've ever wanted that for you."

My heart squeezes tight, because I know that's true. Maybe he wanted to understand me better. Maybe I would have liked to understand him better, but I always knew he wanted what was best for me. "Thank you, Daddy."

"Now give me a tour of this show before the whole world wants a piece of you."

So I show him around the paintings of Medusa's life and death. Only when we get to the final piece do I find Mom standing there, staring at it as if transfixed.

"Hell," Daddy breathes.

Mom turns back with a slight smile. Her dress is glimmering and couture, showing off a figure some twenty-year-olds would kill for. She's always been a beautiful woman, but never a happy one. "Look at what our girl did."

Daddy clears his throat. "She's... incomparable."

Only I don't think he's talking about me.

And for a moment, with both my parents in the same place, not fighting, not throwing anything, with Christopher in the same city and planning to come to my show, everything is perfect. After my childhood I should have known that perfection is only ever an illusion. A shine you put on things that are too broken to ever be fixed.

Chapter Nine
Cautionary Tale

THE ROOM IS packed by the time the curator drags me to the makeshift platform to give a little speech. I give a small wave to my professor, who looks so different in a black lace dress instead of the brown tweed suits she wears to class. Christopher leans against the back wall, looking impeccable in a suit but somehow distant from everyone.

Someone who should belong but doesn't.

I'm not twenty-one yet, but Mom gave me a glass of champagne. It left my throat dry and scratchy, or at least that's how it feels as I look out at mostly strangers. They've been exclaiming and complimenting my work since they showed up.

My central piece is still up for auction.

Those display walls are glorified plywood; they don't even reach the ceiling. The curator was more than willing to take a chunk out of the maze for the publicity. The audience seem to like the whole surprise element of the main portrait, because the auction has already risen to crazy proportions even without Daddy bidding. I'm not sure if it's really the painting they love or the story around it, but either way that's a lot of money for charity.

I grasp the microphone, pretending my hands aren't slick with sweat. Pretending my voice doesn't quaver. "The story goes that Athena cursed Medusa with hair made of snakes and a face so horrible it would turn men to stone. We are told that she did this as a just punishment, because she was so offended that Medusa was raped in her temple. Except how would that be just, to blame Medusa for something that she didn't want and didn't cause?"

The crowd looks back at me, a little aghast, a lot uncomfortable that I would talk about this while they're wearing diamonds that cost the same as a whole car.

"I don't think Athena cursed her, not really. I think she gave Medusa what she wanted most—weapons to protect herself with. Power, when it had been taken from her."

It strikes me then, how close Daddy and Mom are standing next to each other. As if they're a couple, when they could barely stand to talk to each other to arrange visitation.

"Do you know," I ask the crowd, "that there is no recorded instance of her turning a woman to stone? Only men."

Christopher might be made from stone, that's how still he is as he watches me with those mysterious black eyes. It's like he's holding his breath, and maybe he is. Waiting to see how the story ends, even if we think we already know.

"In the end, it wasn't enough. Men found a way to use her, taking her power for themselves, using her head to defeat their enemies. Medusa is a cautionary tale. She always has been, but I don't think she's warning us away from rage." The last words I say directly to Christopher. "She's warning us to use it better. To use it *more*. That's our power, in the end."

The crowd claps for me while Daddy hoots and whistles, because he can't help but show his support for me. It feels like absolute exhilaration, stepping down from the platform and accepting the handshakes and hugs from people around me.

Mom squeezes me in a delicate hug, and Daddy puts his arms around us both. How long has it been since they hugged me at the same time? I can't find a memory to place this with; it's in a box all its own. And then they let me go—too soon.

I find myself standing in front of Christopher, a lingering smile on my lips. Even my embarrassment over the rejection last night can't touch me now. We may not kiss again, but this man is a friend. Maybe the best friend I ever had.

"You blew them away," he says.

"You helped."

He shakes his head. "I'm not taking any credit for lock picking."

"It's a very interesting skill. You'll have to tell me where you picked it up."

His mouth opens, but I don't hear anything. There's a rush in the crowd, a heavy jostle that leaves me unsteady on my green-velvet heels. For a minute I think they must have released fresh trays of champagne from the kitchen. Maybe filled with bonus diamonds?

Until there's a scream from behind me. I whirl to see my mother kneeling on the ground beside Daddy, who has his hand clutched to his heart, his eyes staring up at nothing.

Something dark moves through me, a sense that I caused this somehow. With my paintings or my hopeless dreams. That this is my fault.

"No," I whisper, but I can tell from the sound of my mother's mournful wail, like the sound you hear far away in an untamed desert, haunting and stark, that he's gone.

"Fuck," Christopher says, the word harsh.

My head feels light, and I realize in a split second of surprise that I'm going to faint. That my body would rather shut down than face what's happening. I'm falling, again, and this time there are strong hands to catch me.

CHAPTER TEN
Empty-Handed

THE FUNERAL TAKES place four days later in a historic cathedral in Boston. It's a private affair, with only me and Mom and Christopher and a handful of very close business partners. One of them gives Mom a look of undisguised hunger and makes her promise to let him know if she needs anything. Another one of them gives the same look and extracts the same promise from me.

I walk through the whole thing in a daze. Vaguely I'm aware that I've taken a leave of absence from school, that I should be dealing with grief. And maybe I could, if I could bring myself to really believe that it happened. Mostly I keep waiting to wake up.

Keep waiting for a hand to reach into the water and pull me out.

Christopher doesn't approach me at the funeral.

He doesn't write any more letters.

It's like a second blow, his absence, a fatal one

where my father's death has maimed me. I try not to think about it, the same way I try not to think about Daddy.

While the funeral was a quiet affair, I'm dreading the reading of the will, because it will be a circus. Every single one of his wives and most of his past stepchildren will be in attendance to see if anything was bequeathed to them.

"Please don't make me go."

The words come out as a hoarse murmur, because I've only said them for the millionth time. It's not like my inheritance is a raffle ticket that will be forfeited if I don't show up. The actual will reading is just a formality. An anachronism. A public stoning. Someone will tell me what Daddy gave me, whether it's two dollars or two billion. It doesn't matter whether I'm present at the will reading. And God, I don't want to be there.

Mom sits on the sofa beside me, her eyes rimmed red from crying. She's mourned the loss of him more in the past two weeks than she did in the decade they had been divorced. "You and I are the only ones who deserve to be there."

She thinks he's going to give her something, and it kills me. Could he have changed that much? God, the child support arguments were so bitter. So freaking specific. By the end he had seemed to soften toward her. At the art studio there had been a moment when he'd looked at her and I'd had the thought that every child of divorced parents has at least once, a desperate hope, a terrible dream that they might get back together.

I shake my head. "Neither of us should be there. It will be terrible."

"We hold our heads high. All of those money-hungry bastards can sit there and be embarrassed when it comes out that they aren't getting anything."

And what happens when it comes out that you aren't? "Mom, whatever happens... you know that whatever I have, it's yours. Right?"

"You think he's going to leave me out?"

I look away, at the nondescript painting on the nondescript hotel wall. We're living on borrowed money right now, paying for this hotel room on credit because surely Daddy will have left us money.

Except I'm not so sure.

He loved me; I know that. And he even loved my mom in his own way. But he was always tied up about money. I could see him leaving me nothing as some kind of character-building experiment. I would have to quit Smith College without any way to pay the tuition, but I'm not as worried about me.

I'm more worried about what would happen to my mother's fragile sense of self if she holds her head high against all those wives and then ends up humiliated. She hasn't even met most of them. I've met them, on my annual spring break visits.

There would be glee, to see the first and most coveted wife taken down.

"I just think it doesn't make sense to put ourselves through that. Everyone's going to see someone else get taken down."

"They're going because they think they were important to him."

I'm not sure Daddy was that black-and-white. He cared for his other wives; at least he didn't treat them with disdain. But they got their small piece of their fortune with the ironclad prenup he made them sign. He won't give them more than that, but not for the reasons that Mom thinks.

The other children will be there, too. Not biological children. I'm the only one he had, but there are plenty of other stepchildren through the years.

Including Christopher. *Will he be there?*

It will kill me to see him salivating for Daddy's fortune. Except why wouldn't he? He's always wanted money, and Daddy's money is as good as any.

"Whatever happens, we'll be okay," I say, but I'm not sure who I'm trying to convince.

Mom gives a firm shake of her head. "He wouldn't leave us empty-handed."

CHAPTER ELEVEN

Liquid and Otherwise

THE WILL READING takes place at my father's lawyer's office, which is on the thirty-eighth floor of a building that overlooks a park blooming with pink and white cherry blossoms. It's strange to see the world so full of life when we're wearing black and facing death.

Mr. Smith, that's the name of the lawyer. A plain name for a rather plain man. He looks like he would follow the letter of the law down any path it would take him. Quite the rule follower, and it makes sense that Daddy would have used him for this purpose. Lord knows there are a large group of people who would love to contest even the smallest loophole. It's standing room only, the wood door propped open to let wives seven and eight peek their heads in from the hallway.

It's actually as much of a circus as I feared, with my mother and me being granted the dubious honor of the two chairs in front of the desk. It also means everyone can watch us.

Christopher is here, standing in the corner, looking as if he'd like to be anywhere but here—which must be a lie, because he didn't have to come. Unless he wants the fortune.

Acid burns my throat. So, he's as money hungry as everyone in this room. I wish I didn't know that about him. It would have been better not to come, if only to avoid facing that fact.

That Christopher wants Daddy's fortune.

"Thank you for gathering today," Mr. Smith says in a voice dry as leaves in the fall. "While many wills are handled via mail, this is a rather unusual case. I have asked any interested parties to attend so that we may all have closure and put an end to the numerous inquiries to the firm."

In other words the phone must be ringing off the hook with people wanting some of Daddy's money. My stomach feels inside out. Did he know what kind of mess he would leave behind? He must have thought about it when he wrote whatever's on that piece of paper the lawyer's holding. Did he think of how it would feel to be surrounded by so many ex-wives and stepsiblings, all of whom are essentially strangers?

Did he know that Mom would be holding her head high, certain he would stand by her in the end? I sure as hell hope so. We're about to find out in the most public way.

A violent, hacking clearing of the throat. And then Mr. Smith begins to read. "If you're reading this, that means I'm finally at peace. And though I'll miss a good many things on this earth, one of them won't be the exorbitant amount of money I've paid lawyers over the years."

There's a nervous laugh from the side that's abruptly silenced.

In the same monotone Mr. Smith continues, "To the son that I never had, Christopher Bardot, I bequeath *Liquid Asset* as well as a small trust with which to care for her. I wish we could have sailed together more than once."

I'm jolted out of my grief-stricken stupor at the sound of his name. A ripple of excitement runs through the room. Christopher isn't his biological child, which means there's hope for everyone else in this room.

"As for the rest of my assets, both liquid and otherwise," Mr. Smith reads, "I bequeath them in entirety to my daughter, Harper St. Claire."

There's a gasp in the room, and I'm painfully aware of the looks of pure venom being shot in my direction. All I can do is stare straight ahead, shocked at hearing my father's final words, even if spoken in a voice so unlike his own. It's strange that hollowness can feel so solid, a physical sensation that threatens to bend me at the waist. *Daddy, come back.*

Nothing is so cold and so calculating as money in a void where love and hope had been. I don't want his billions of dollars, or however much his fortune amounts to. I never did. If there's one upside in all of this, it's that Mom will finally be able to relax. A small comfort.

"I have a stipulation for Harper, who is still young and impressionable as I write this. The money will be placed into a trust, which will only transfer to her when she turns twenty-five."

A heavy hum of conversation pierces my haze. That's seven years away. Seven years before I can return to Smith College. Seven years before my mother can stop marrying whoever will have her.

"Of course I don't want to cause undue burden to her, so she may access money as needed for her education and living situation. But only for her. No one else may use the money, including my ex-wife."

"No," I say, my voice rusty. "Stop."

He can't do this to her, not in front of all these people. How can he humiliate her this way? He must have known. God, he must have known.

Mr. Smith gives me a pitying look before

reading on. "To that end I name Christopher Bardot as the executor of the trust. I know that he will make sure my wishes are honored and that my only daughter is well cared for in my absence."

The paper has barely brushed the gleaming wooden surface of the desk when the room erupts into chaos. There are demands to confirm the validity of the will, insistence that they will contest it. When I bring myself to look sideways, I see my mother has turned to stone—she's frozen in place, a look of polite acceptance on her face.

It's too horrible.

I grab her hand and drag her from the room, pushing through people I don't even recognize in my quest to reach the wide marble hallway. How are we even going to find a taxi in this mess? We'll be flagged down, caught on camera. This is what rich people have bodyguards for, but we're not rich regardless of what just happened in that lawyer's office. We have nothing, maybe not even a way to pay the hotel bill. I spin in the hallway, useless. There's nowhere to run.

Christopher appears out of nowhere. "Come on, there's a car waiting."

I'm too frantic to even ask a question, like where we're going. He could say we're driving into the depths of hell, and I'd probably still follow him, taking Mom by the hand, pulling us both into the cocoon of a darkened limo. The press see us as Christopher moves to step inside, running toward us with their microphones outstretched and video cameras hot on their heels as the door shuts. Then the limo eases forward, taking us far away.

"Thank you," I say, feeling both numb and exhilarated.

Christopher glances out the back window, his expression grim. "Damn him," he mutters. "He should have given you some warning at least."

Damn him. I cling to those two words like they're a life preserver. Like when Christopher helped me break into the artist studio. We're together, aren't we? "You won't help him, will you?"

My mother runs a shaky hand through her hair. "I'm ruined. No one will have me after this. Half the town knows what happened by now. There's probably a YouTube video."

I hate that she's right. Daddy did more than make sure she couldn't get his money. In that one public moment he made sure she would never marry well again. Everyone will say there must be something wrong with her, for Daddy to omit her this way. She'll be the laughingstock of high society. Those rich husbands of hers, they didn't only marry her body. They married her position in society. Her connections. The way she could host a dinner party with senators and billionaires. It doesn't matter if I become a world-renowned artist, my mother will never get another society invitation again.

The limo turns onto the highway and speeds up. I'm sitting next to my mother, and I reach across the supple leather to take her hand in mine. Across from us Christopher looks haggard. He stares out the tinted window where the city speeds by.

I squeeze my mother's hand. "It will be okay."

"How?" Her mouth forms the word, but no sound comes out.

"Christopher will help us," I say, the words like a tether. The red and white life preserver for me to hold on to when it's too hard to swim. He's always been there when I need him. Why would this time be any different? "He's the executor, so he's the one who decides what counts as being for me or for you. He'll make sure you're taken care of."

God knows there's enough money in that trust fund to take care of my mother twenty times over, in the most extravagant ways she can think up. I didn't expect Daddy to leave me empty-handed, necessarily, but I also didn't expect to get every terrible cent.

The entire St. Claire fortune, minus the yacht.

I look at Christopher, but he hasn't moved. I might as well have turned him to granite, the same way I did to my father at the exhibit. I don't feel like I'm cursed and full of rage. My dirty-blonde hair doesn't slither and hiss, but the men around me are as cold and hard as stone.

"You'll help us, won't you? It's too cruel, what Daddy did. It's wrong. If the money is mine, I can spend it however I want. Why shouldn't Mom get some of it?"

It won't matter if none of the rich assholes who think they own the world will marry my mother, not if she's already taken care of. It will hurt her to be shunned by her so-called friends, but at least she'll be able to live comfortably.

The strong profile and ebony hair does not move a single centimeter even as the limo exits the freeway and turns toward our hotel. Through the windshield I can see a small crowd gathered at the front door. The press. Not the hard-hitting journalism that exposed the corruption at my old school after my Medusa painting. These are the tabloid freelancers and gossip bloggers. We aren't celebrities in the way that a musician or a model is, but everyone likes to see the rich brought low. They've come to gloat at my mother's pain.

"Christopher!"

He speaks in a low voice to the driver, who turns before we reach the crowd. There's already a uniformed cop waiting to direct us into the parking garage. An entrance for celebrities and politicians, I realize. Someone set this up ahead of time. A way into the building without having to run the gauntlet of paparazzi.

Someone who knew we would need this.

"You," I whisper, my chest crushed by a thousand-pound weight.

Christopher finally looks at me, and I can't contain my gasp as I see the resignation in his eyes. "It's his last request, Harper. The only thing he ever asked of me. How can I say no?"

CHAPTER TWELVE

Inheritance

IT TAKES ME forty-five minutes and a Valium to get my mother to relax in her bedroom, her lashes still damp from tears of anxiety and grief. Light batters my eyes as I step out of her bedroom and close the door gently behind me.

"Have you always taken care of her like that?" Christopher asks from the large windows that frame the city, his hands behind his back, looking out.

How dare he judge? He doesn't know her, or he wouldn't even be considering doing what Daddy asked him to do. And he doesn't know me, if he thinks I would speak to him ever again. "I'm sorry that not everyone in the world can live up to your exacting standards. I suppose we should all be so heartless as to put money before family."

He glances back, his eyes flashing. "Is that what I'm doing?"

If I were smart, I'd heed the warning in his

voice, but he's the one with the GPA and the plans to take over the world. I'm the troublemaker. "Aren't you?"

A hollow laugh. "Is that why you think I stopped kissing you that night at the studio? Because you're my stepsister? Because I think of you like family?"

The way he says *family* it might as well mean *nuclear waste.* "I mean, yeah. But now I think maybe it was something else."

Those black eyes that hold so many secrets, they look over my body from the top to the bottom with such slow, obvious hunger that it seems impossible I would not have seen it before. "You aren't my sister, Harper St. Claire. And I have never, not once, thought of you that way."

My skin lights up under his stark perusal. "Then how do you think of me?"

He stalks forward until my back hits the wall of the suite. "Like you're the daughter of the only man who ever gave a damn about me." His mouth is only two inches away from mine...an inch...and then I can feel the gentle caress of his breath against my lips. "You were completely off-limits, when he was alive—" A rough sound. "And even more so now that he's gone and asked me to do this thing that will make you hate me."

"Then don't do it," I beg softly, and it's almost a kiss, my lips moving near his.

"You have no idea, Harper. No idea what you're asking me."

"He was wrong to make that rule!"

"Maybe so, but I don't know what the hell happened between your mom and him. It's not my place to judge whether he should have done it or not. It's his money, and this is how he wants it spent."

"It's *my* money," I say, my voice made imperious with impotent rage.

He huffs his amusement. "Spoken like a true St. Claire."

"Christopher, I don't know if you think we're only in this for billions of dollars. I don't care about that. We have nothing. *She has nothing.* All she needs is enough to live off of. You can have the rest."

He steps back as if I slapped him. "You think I want your inheritance?"

Something wavers inside me. Did I go too far? Christopher is going to let my mother starve because he wants to honor a request that should never have been made. That's wrong. Not me standing up for her. "Everyone else in that room wanted it. And you were there."

It's like watching ice form over a lake in a matter of seconds. The water had seemed deep and unnerving, but now he's simply impenetrable. "The only reason I went to that damn reading is because the lawyer called me this morning and said I should come. And something in his voice told me it was going to be bad, so I had the car waiting for us and the hotel on standby."

My throat feels scratchy, like I'm near tears. "I didn't thank you for that."

"I don't want your thanks. I don't want that fucking yacht, either. And I sure as hell don't want a single cent from your inheritance."

"We've been living in a motel." The words burst out of me, ugly and hushed so my mother doesn't wake up. "Every day Mom takes one of her jewelry pieces to the pawn shop, where they give her a few cents for every dollar that it's really worth. That's how we pay the bill so we have a place to sleep that night."

My words crack the ice around him, at least enough so that I see the old Christopher looking back at me, the one who would have dived into the ocean to save me. "Hell."

"Daddy paid for my tuition and my private dorm room directly, but that's it. If I had asked for anything more, he would have had his investigators look into us again."

He shakes his head. "I don't understand."

The words spill from me, more careless with our secrets than I've ever been. No, not careless. Trusting him to do what's right. "When I was nine, Mom was between husbands. We had this shitty apartment on the outskirts of LA and ate ramen noodles every night. It sucked, but I didn't really care. But I cared when Mom said we couldn't afford to get more paint, so I called Daddy." Tears sting my eyes, and it's such a twisted feeling to mourn him right now, to love him and hate him at the same time. "He came down on us like freaking Zeus from Mount Olympus. He took me to New York City until she had enough money to come get me, and that was only when she had found this asshole director who wanted her as his side piece. She did that for *me*, so that I could come back."

Christopher stares at me as if testing the words, weighing them the way he must weigh every sentence spoken in his crazy-smart Emerson business classes, the way he must gauge everything around him with that stone-cold confidence. And he must see in me the desperate truth, because he stalks back to the window and curses under his breath.

He's not even facing me, but I'm utterly and completely exposed. I could strip naked in this suite and still not be as naked as I feel right now. This is something I don't talk about with anyone, least of all with a man who's saved me twice. It's something of a pattern already, and that should be enough for me to make it stop. I can't depend on anyone, even him.

But I can't let my mother go back to arguing with the landlord for a few extra days. Not when I'm living like a princess at Smith College in the dorm Daddy paid extra to get. I can't let her whore herself to some asshole with money when I'm the heiress to a freaking fortune.

If I've convinced Christopher, the shame I'm feeling would have been worth it.

Please let it be enough.

He faces me, and he's so fully Christopher, so much the person standing beside me with his forearms on the railing that I breathe a sigh of relief. This man, I know him. He's the one I can count on to catch me when I'm falling.

"Harper," he says. My throat squeezes. He sounds like he's facing a firing squad. "Maybe it's wrong to use this against you, but you told me about that husband, the one who owned the job website. The one who climbed into your bed. And that makes me think your dad was right."

"No," I whisper, because this isn't going to end the way I hoped.

"He knew, okay? Your father knew that I'm a man of my word. He knew how much that meant to me… and why it means so much to me."

"Why?" I whisper, even though I know he isn't going to tell me. This is a man who hoards secrets the way a dragon keeps gold and jewels in his lair.

I would rather have no money than have a trust fund I can't use to support my mother… which Daddy probably knew, too. It was a final *fuck you* to the woman he could never get over. I accepted that weakness from Daddy a long time ago, but having him use Christopher to do it makes my stomach turn over.

I would be pissed, my friend had said once. *Like he's trying to control you with money, even though he has so much.* And for the first time I do feel pissed.

"He appointed me as the executor, and not the hundred other men he knows could have done it. Because he knew I would have to do it, if he asked me. And that I would never take a single cent out of the damn trust fund for myself or anyone else."

"Isn't there something more important than keeping your word? Isn't there doing what's right?"

A dark laugh. "Not to me."

"Don't do this."

He's made of stone again, any semblance of vulnerability turned hard. "It's already done, Harper. It was done before today. Before the art studio. It was done when your father sat down and wrote the will, knowing exactly what would happen."

"You're giving him all the power." All the power to ruin whatever was between us. That kiss standing beneath Medusa's wrathful gaze. Maybe we had been doomed from the beginning.

"It's not his choice anymore, Harper. Not even yours. It's mine. And I'm going to do this for you, because he asked me to, and because it's the only way I can protect you, even from yourself. You'll give away every cent if you think it will help someone."

"Protect me? This isn't the Massachusetts Bay! I'm not sitting on the damn rail."

"You told me to leave you alone then, too. And I'll never regret staying on deck so that I could dive in after you. I'll do it again if I have to."

What would it take for this man to see me as a woman? As someone that can make her own decisions instead of as a maiden who needs saving. But I don't think it's even about me or what I need. He already told me, didn't he? It's his choice, and he would rather be a white knight whether it helps me or not.

"Christopher," I say, my voice low and desperate. "That kiss."

His black eyes sharpen. "What about it?"

"It means something to me." Even if I have to slash my skin to pieces. That's how much Christopher is worth to me. It's more than a girlish crush, the way I feel about him. The feelings that are wavering like a drop of water on a petal, about to slide away.

"I told you it was a mistake."

I swallow hard. "I think you're lying. I think it meant something to you, too."

His eyes are more opaque than ever, obsidian and shining. He twists his mouth into a look that's worse than dislike—into pity. "You're young, but I didn't think you were stupid. A kiss doesn't mean anything."

My father's death should have been enough to break me, but somehow I was whole. Until now, when I'm in a million pieces at Christopher

Bardot's feet. "No."

"I felt bad for you, to be honest. That's why I wrote you back."

"You're lying," I say, hating the tears in my eyes.

"You weren't a sister to me." His words are cold, his eyes unfeeling. There's no doubt he means those words. "You meant nothing to me. Just a poor little rich girl, all along."

Betrayal knots itself in my stomach, so tight and so deep I'm not sure I'll ever be free of it. "Then why don't you walk away, if I mean so little? Let me manage the trust fund, and you never have to talk to me again."

"Obligation. This is something I have to do out of respect for your father."

Not out of respect for me. Never that.

Both men and money have a way of disappearing when you need them most. It's something I learned early, but clearly I needed to learn it again. Neither my stepbrother nor the inheritance were anything I could count on.

Neither of them were anything I could trust.

CHAPTER THIRTEEN

Business Partner

THE PAPER IN my hand has been crushed in my fist and smoothed out with shaking hands so many times the ink has almost faded. Almost, but I have the words memorized anyway.

"Where is he?" I ask the pretty receptionist without introducing myself. It must be obvious who I am, unless Christopher Bardot likes to torment women all over the country. He might have given her a heads-up; Like, "by the way, I have a stepsister who hates my guts." Maybe they laugh about it before she gives him a blow job from beneath his desk.

That seems like exactly the kind of thing he would do.

"He's in a meeting," she says, clearly planning to block me. But her eyes give her away, her gaze darting to the frosted-glass doors to her right.

"Don't bother buzzing me in," I tell her, already heading in that direction.

When I push open the door, I'm confronted

by a large conference room with dark wood paneling and leather chairs. There's only one man inside.

And it's not him.

Where Christopher's hair is dark, this man's is a deep gold, as if it's been turned that way from hours spent in the sun. Instead of eyes black like obsidian, this man has blue eyes that look as bright as the sky on a hot summer day.

In so many ways they're opposite, but there's something about him that's similar. The strength inherent in their bodies. The hunger for more than what he has. I recognize an ambitious man the way a gazelle lifts her head and senses a tiger nearby.

This man takes his time examining my body. I shiver a little in the cool office air, goose bumps on my skin. It's only the air-conditioning that makes my nipples turn hard beneath the cotton T-shirt, at least I think so, but it's embarrassing either way.

"May I help you?" he says, and in those four words I hear a deep Southern drawl. While his eyes express acute interest, his tone is considerably more reserved.

"I'm looking for Christopher Bardot." My voice comes out strong, which is impressive when you consider the carnal appetite in this man's eyes would make a siren blush. If I weren't riding high on righteous anger I'd probably stammer and stumble like every other female of the species must do when faced with a man as clearly alpha as this one. Some evolutionary instinct grabs hold of my ovaries and says, *this man will hunt and protect and fuck.*

"He's not in the office at the moment, but if you want to sit down a spell, you can tell me what he's done to piss you off. Maybe there's something I can do to help."

"Do you have a piñata shaped like him and a bat? That would help."

He stares at me for a moment, and I think he's about to throw me out on the street. That would probably be the right thing to do considering he doesn't know who I am. Instead he throws his head back and laughs. "I like your spirit, even if I can't condone your methods. My business partner has many annoying qualities, but even so, I would like him intact."

"Your business partner?"

"Sutton Mayfair," he says, standing as he introduces himself with old-world manners. There are stacks of papers surrounding him on the glossy conference table. Clearly I've interrupted him at work, but he doesn't look impatient in the least. There's something deceptively casual about him in his slightly rumpled suit and blond hair an inch too long. The kind of deception that would make his enemies underestimate him.

"So you must know where I can find him."

"You can leave a message at the front desk."

"And lose the element of surprise? I'd rather not."

A small smile. "I know where he'll be tonight. There's some party happening, and we're supposed to go. I wasn't looking forward to wearing a penguin suit for the rich and powerful in Tanglewood, but the evening will be a whole lot more interesting if you're there."

My eyes narrow in suspicion. "Why would you help me?"

"Perhaps I want to see you in an evening dress."

I've been asked out a hundred times before, but never with the blunt self-assurance that this man conveys. It's a strange combination of courtesy and outright lust. "Are you taking advantage of the situation, Sutton?"

His blue eyes dance with humor. "I'm an opportunist, and I think you might be one too."

"Fine, I'll take it."

"I'd much rather pick you up. Maybe have dinner first."

Have a date with Christopher's business partner? He would probably have a heart attack at the idea that anyone would treat me as a woman instead of a child. "A gentleman would add my name to the guest list."

"Did I give you the impression that I was a gentleman? My apologies."

"Now I can see why Christopher went into business with you."

He places a hand on his heart, and even a few yards away I can see the roughened skin of him, the calluses and the faint white scars. Those are the hands of a working man, for all that he wears a suit and works in a high-rise now. "Ruthless," he says.

"If that means I have my own invitation to the party." There's something alluring about Sutton Mayfair. If I met him in New York City, if he asked me out in a bar, I would say yes. But I can't trust him knowing he's tied to Christopher Bardot. Not even for one night.

Really, there's no end to the things Christopher will ruin for me.

"On one condition," he says. "Show me what you're holding."

The paper. I'm wearing my power boots and a T-shirt that says, *Feminist AF*. Of course he would have noticed my one weakness. It's the reason I'm here in this office. Here in Tanglewood. The reason I need an invitation to the party tonight.

Swallowing down my shame, I toss the crumpled ball onto the cherrywood. He picks it up and smooths it out, his large fingers unerringly gentle with the worried bill.

"Looks like someone didn't pay this," he says, one square-tipped finger running down the credit card statement. I have a prickling sensation that tells me he would be able to recite its entire contents despite his good-old-boy demeanor.

"And that someone will have to answer to me. Tonight."

He folds the paper carefully in half, and then half again. When he hands it back, it's almost completely flat. "Do you need money?"

"I have money." Not the ability to spend it— one of life's ironies.

He takes a step toward me, and suddenly I'm taking a step back. How did this man go from accommodating to dangerous in one second flat? "Christopher mentioned you."

My mouth feels dry. I tell myself I don't care about what Christopher says, that I don't care what this man thinks of me. "Did he?"

"He made you sound about this high. A child."

There's acid in my throat. "Of course."

"Now that I see you, I think he was holding out on me." Those blue eyes look at more than just my body; they look inside me, finding the sensitive places—pressing on them, only a little. Enough to make me gasp when his gaze catches mine.

"I'm not a child," I say, which only serves to make me sound like a child.

"No," he says, his lips forming the word, almost soundless. "Do you think Christopher is really confused about that? Do you think he sees that mouth and doesn't imagine all the things he could do to it? Do you think he doesn't think about you when he comes?"

My cheeks warm. "How dare you."

He gives me a smile that can only be described as indecent. "Maybe he is that blind."

I follow his stark blue gaze down to my chest, where my nipples have become hard at the *E* and the *A*. Even while my mind denies what this man is saying to me, my body already agrees. Christopher has always treated me like a child, but this man... he knows I'm a woman.

"There can't be anything between us. I hate your business partner."

"You think that's a requirement for being my lover? Come to the gala tonight. Make him suffer all you want, as long as you don't go home with him at the end of the night."

Surprise steals my breath, along with an unnerving rush of arousal. It's pure heat between my legs, the opposite of the ice-cold Christopher leaves me with. Who knew I would find the caveman thing so hot? I blame evolution, an ages-old certainty that this man could protect me from saber-tooth tigers. "You have no right to say that."

He gives me a half smile that doesn't quite dispute my words. *Not yet,* it seems to say instead. A caveman he might be, but he also has a sense of determined patience. Too bad I've had my share of men with ambition. Whether they're brooding and reserved like Christopher or confident and possessive like this one, they have no place in my world.

CHAPTER FOURTEEN

Old-Money Girls

"I'VE HEARD THE strangest rumor," says the familiar voice over the phone, "that my best friend is in the city. I said there's no way because she didn't tell me she was visiting."

I stare up at the crystal and gold chandelier that hangs above me, set in a thick crown molding. I'm staying at L'Etoile, a boutique hotel in downtown. "I'm sorry I didn't tell you, but it's complicated."

"So it's about your stepbrother."

"You didn't tell me he moved to Tanglewood."

She's quiet a moment, and I know the accusation came out in my voice too strong. "I wasn't sure he'd stick around, but Harper... he's going to be in your life. There's no escaping that, at least until you turn twenty-five."

"And not a second too soon." I've mostly managed to avoid the trust fund altogether, besides the payments to Smith College, which were sent automatically.

It's obscene the amount of money sitting in a bank account under my name. It's only gotten bigger under Christopher's careful stewardship, his investments making me one of the richest women in the country. The man knows how to turn money into more money, that's for sure. The Midas touch. I could buy a castle on every continent if I wanted one, but I can't even write a check to charity.

The biggest upside to graduating this past spring was never having to touch the trust fund again. Until the credit card bill was an exception to the rule. A time when I had actually needed the trust fund and the ridiculous amount of money inside it.

Naturally, that means I couldn't have it.

"I'm at the Emerald," she says, referring to the gorgeous old hotel that Gabriel Miller bought her near Smith College while she goes to grad school. "But you can still stay at our place. I can call the security firm to let you in."

"Nah, I like L'Etoile. The way they've bastardized everything beautiful appeals to me."

She laughs softly and then sobers. "How's your mom?"

"In remission," I say, my throat tight.

"If you need help…" The offer hangs in the air, sharp enough to leave scratch marks on my skin. "You were there for me when my father was sick. Don't think I've forgotten that."

"And you didn't take a cent from me."

"Harper."

"We're managing," I tell her softly, which is mostly true. My paintings are just shocking enough to sell for large sums of money through my Etsy shop, usually sold a few minutes after I post them on my Instagram account. That money has supported me and my mother, but the medical bills are a little too intense for even a bloodthirsty Calypso.

"Have you talked to Christopher?"

"Tonight. I have an invitation to the Tangle-wood Historical Society's Annual Gala."

She groans. "You're going to run the gauntlet?"

"It was the only way I could find him. He wasn't at his office." I hesitate, a little uncertain whether I want to ask the next question. There's something intimate about my encounter there, more intimate than it should seem for talking to a stranger with the conference room door open. "Have you met Sutton Mayfair?"

"No, but I've heard about him. He's new on

the scene, so naturally all the old-money girls are obsessed with him." Her voice turns speculative. "Apparently he's very sexy."

"If you like that Southern-boy charm." Which apparently I do? I haven't had much exposure to that in LA or New York City, but turns out it's seductive in a visceral way. It was easy to friendzone the artists at Smith College. Easy to roll my eyes at the ambitious business students, enough like Christopher Bardot to make me hate them on sight.

Harder to ignore the masculine confidence inherent in Sutton Mayfair.

"It's more than an act. He grew up on a ranch, so you know..." Her voice sounds like pure wickedness as the words trail off.

"So he likes mucking stalls?"

"He's probably good with rope, I was going to say."

That makes me laugh when I didn't think it was possible, not in my current mood. This is why Avery is my best friend. She can make me laugh even when I'm walking the figurative plank over a circle of rabid sharks. "I'm absolutely one hundred percent positive I won't be finding out whether he's good with rope."

"Never say never."

I remember the heat in his blue-sky eyes and shiver with remembered response. "I'm going to the gala to see Christopher. I doubt I'll even talk to Sutton there, especially if he has the old-money girls flipping their hair to get him into bed."

"Okay," she says cheerfully, clearly not believing a word.

"And even if I did talk to him, I have no interest in going to bed with some overmuscled Neanderthal who looks amazing in a suit. I like my men more… enlightened."

"Mhmm. I'm going to have someone send over this dress I ordered online but haven't worn yet. It's red and shimmery and it will look incredible on you."

"I don't need a dress," I say, even though absolutely nothing in my canvas carry-on is suitable for a gala. There are sundresses and skinny jeans and paint-splattered pj's.

"Text me when you get home, or I'll worry about you."

"You're just hoping I give you dirty details, but there won't be anything dirty. There's only going to be me telling Christopher he's an arrogant jerk face, and him bending to my will."

She laughs. "Okay, but text me anyway."

The dress arrives an hour later, even more

gorgeous than she made it sound. There's a red silk bodice that makes my modest breasts look impressive in the ornate gold-plated wall mirror. And a black wrap skirt that floats around me like liquid when I walk, revealing an impressive amount of leg. It's a dress that a modern-day goddess would wear, along with the black and red Louboutins included in the box. In short I'm dressed to kill.

CHAPTER FIFTEEN

Teardown and Rebuild

THE GALA TAKES place in the Tanglewood Country Club, a place that charges enough money to its members that the carpet shouldn't look quite as shabby as it does. It's a place with more clout than taste, which probably says more about the historical society than they think.

I can hear the gentle hum of voices and clink of glasses from down the hallway. The suited security guard makes me wait while he searches a printed guest list, which I'm not on. Do they really have a problem with party crashers hungry for dry quiche and dry conversation? Maybe it's been too long since we moved in wealthy circles, because my hands start to sweat. I don't belong here, at least not in spirit, and even this random stranger knows it.

Only when he uses his phone to check his e-mail does he find my late addition.

Holding my head high, I stride through the room. Avery grew up in Tanglewood, so I'm guessing she knows most of the people in this room. I know basically no one, and I don't see Christopher anywhere.

There are admiring looks because of the amazing dress.

Curious looks, because of my anonymity.

A familiar drawl slows my step. "Not sure it's better falling down," Sutton says, his back turned to me, speaking to an older woman who clearly does not appreciate his words.

"The Tanglewood Library has an important history, and it's the job of the society to preserve that. We aren't going to give it to just anyone who moves in with money."

"It hasn't been given away, Mrs. Rosemont. I bought it."

Her face flushes red, and I realize I've stumbled into the scene that every single person will be talking about in Tanglewood tomorrow morning. Unless I somehow stop it.

"Do you think money counts for everything, young man? You'll find that money can't buy you everything. It can't buy you a construction permit if we tell city hall not to give you one."

"He bought it because he values the foundation," I say, tucking my hand through Sutton's arm as if I belong there. He stiffens only slightly but doesn't give me away. "Maintaining the historical integrity is an important part of the Mayfair-Bardot corporate philosophy. They plan to work closely with the society to ensure they do it justice."

Her eyes narrow. "Then why haven't they contacted us before now?"

I shake my head, commiserating with her at the cluelessness of men. "They've been overly focused on things like paperwork and permits. That's why they're here tonight, though. To meet you and ask for your help in doing this the right way."

"I see." She looks pissed, but at least she stops threatening him. "The gala is hardly the place to discuss details."

Sutton clears his throat. "We would be happy to host you at our offices at your earliest convenience. We wouldn't dream of moving forward without the society's input."

"You need more than our input," the woman says sharply. "You need our approval or you'll never get the construction permits you need from the mayor's office."

I manage to keep a straight face, even though it's painfully clear that Sutton and Christopher had planned to move forward without the society's input. It may not have even occurred to them that the society might object—or that they could put in place roadblocks with building permits. I may not know the specifics of Tangle-wood, but I know high society. Even if the society itself doesn't have any power, the husbands of its members certainly do.

Sutton manages to use that Southern charm to win Mrs. Rosemont over, so that she's blushing and trying not to smile by the time she's called away by another woman.

"You saved me," he murmurs the second we're alone.

The words startle me, because I'm so used to being the one who needs saving. The one who gets saved again and again, even when I don't want that. It's an illicit delight, being the one who does the saving. No wonder Christopher likes it so much. "You would have figured it out."

"I'm a lot better with a construction crew than I am with women."

Considering the looks he's getting from around the room, he's underestimating himself. Even so I have to admit he wasn't doing so well when I found him. "Were you really planning on restoring a historical site without consulting anyone?"

"It was less of a restoration, more of a teardown and rebuild."

I groan. "City hall is going to block you so fast."

"We own the deed," he drawls.

"And they own the city. You can fight them, but that's a last resort. Especially for people who are new to the city like you. It's going to take a while before you have friends."

He looks at me, mystified. "You made friends with that woman."

"That's because I'm interested in people more than money. You should try it sometime."

A rough laugh, the kind I can imagine beneath a vivid sunset in the country. "It's always the people who come from money who think it doesn't matter."

"It's always the ambitious ones that crush everyone in their way."

He pulls me close, and only then do I realize I'm still holding his arm. That we're locked together in the middle of the ballroom. Everyone is looking at us and pretending not to see. They'll be talking about the mystery woman tomorrow. "Then I had better keep you nearby, so you can protect everyone."

My throat tightens. The idea that I can protect anyone… even metaphorically, it's completely absurd. I'm the helpless one, aren't I? At least that's how Christopher Bardot sees me.

A shiver runs through me. I turn to find him behind me, as if conjured from my thoughts. I yank my hand away from Sutton, which only makes me look guilty. I wasn't doing anything wrong. I'm allowed to be here, but Christopher always makes me feel like a troublesome child.

"There you are," I say lamely.

His eyes are narrowed on me. "What are you doing here?"

"Looking for you. You must have known I would come."

"A phone call would have worked."

"Not when it's my mother's health we're talking about."

"We should discuss this in private." He turns to Sutton, and his eyes somehow grow even colder. "How did she even know I would be here?"

Sutton gives a small smile, completely undisturbed by his business partner's fury. "You didn't tell me she was skilled in diplomacy. She already smoothed things over with the historical society."

"For now," I say.

He studies me, as if looking at me through

fresh eyes. Almost. The speculation is gone in a second, leaving only the cold remoteness I know so well. "Follow me," he says, turning and leaving me to trail behind him.

Sutton holds out his arm, and I realize he's going to come with us.

Or at least he's offering to escort me. Does he think I need backup? Looking at his face, I realize he doesn't. It's something far more base. Male possession, except he's asking my permission.

One of these men sees me as competent. The other as a helpless girl. One sees me as powerful. The other as weak. I put my hand in Sutton's arm and walk side by side out of the ballroom, confirming the suspicion of everyone at the gala. They'll all be certain we're together, and the crazy thing is, I'm not sure they're wrong.

Chapter Sixteen

A Tea Party

WE FIND A private room with a handful of old chairs and a fireplace. How many corrupt deals were forged between these four walls? How much money changed hands?

Christopher stands in the corner by the window, his back turned toward us. What does he see? Is he like some conquering warrior, looking at what he plans to take?

In contrast Sutton takes a seat near the fire, one leg slung over the other. His pose is casual, but I'm not fooled. His blue eyes are watchful. He's a powerful adversary, but I'm not sure who he's opposing. Christopher? Or me? Maybe the both of us.

We might be enemies, all three of us.

"You stopped payment to the hospital," I say without preamble. He knows what he did. "I honestly thought you couldn't sink any lower, but you proved me wrong."

"It's not that simple," Christopher says, his

expression grave.

"In case you're wondering, I would have asked for Daddy's help with this if he were alive. And you know what? He would have said yes, so don't pretend this is the high road."

"The instructions didn't leave any ambiguity."

"And you're such a rule follower, are you? You didn't even contact the Tanglewood Historical Society when tearing down a historical property."

"I follow the rules when I agree with them."

My mouth drops open. "You don't agree with helping my mom beat cancer?"

"Hell," he bites out. "That money wasn't going toward medicine. You were buying a butterfly garden for the hospital. And what was that going to get her? A California king-sized hospital bed? A marble bathroom? A doctor to wait on her hand and foot like a goddamned pool boy?"

"I hate you." Not the most logical and persuasive argument, but there's something about Christopher that always cuts through my defenses. He turns me into the wild child that he thinks I am, no matter that years have passed since that night on the yacht.

He runs a hand over his face. "I'm not a monster. I cut off the hospital from taking any more *installments* from you, but I made sure there was a card on file for her medical expenses."

"Your personal credit card."

"Does it matter?"

"I'm not letting you pay for her medicine. We don't need your charity. It's my responsibility, and it will be paid for with my money. As soon as you call the bank and tell them to lift the hold."

Christopher stares at me, and I feel my stomach drop. I know determination when I see it, and it's there in spades in his cold, black eyes. He's not going to budge, but neither am I. We're at an impasse, the same one we've been in since that night in New York City.

Sutton clears his throat. "It's quite a moral dilemma you've got yourself."

"She finds herself in those often," Christopher says.

"I was talking to you," Sutton says in that slow drawl that smooths his sharp words, a flowing stream over sharp rocks. "I knew you were mercenary, but this is cold even for you."

Christopher gives him a sardonic look. "Is there any reason you're here or do you just like seeing me at my worst?"

I'm mildly appeased to hear that I'm the reason for his worst days, but he looks remarkably composed if that's true. Remarkably put together in his tux and shiny shoes. He fits into this room better than Sutton does, better than I do, even if he doesn't respect the order of things.

"I have a solution to propose," Sutton says. "Something that might appease everyone in the room. We need someone to smooth things over with the historical society. Neither you nor I have the time or the ability to make nice with them."

Christopher barks a laugh that makes me flinch. "You're not suggesting Harper."

"Why is that so hard to believe?" I ask, stung more than I should be. Nothing he says should matter to me. It's a weakness that it does. "That someone thinks I'm good for something more than shopping or spa days?"

Christopher blinks, looking, for maybe the first time in his life, uncertain. "Is that how you think I see you? You're a talented artist, Harper."

"And I'm stuck begging for my mother's life."

"She's in remission."

"How would you know that?"

Sutton leans forward, drawing my attention away from the man I want to throttle. Unlike Christopher he doesn't look unmoved by my mother's situation. Instead there's a notch of concern between his eyes. "So she is in remission?"

"For now." There's a sense of relief, however brief, that someone other than me worries about Mom. That particular load, I've carried since I was six years old.

"Good." He relaxes again, as if he cares about what happens to her. And maybe he does. That's a normal trait, concern for your fellow human beings. "We have a lot poured into this recon-struction. Everything we have, in fact."

Christopher makes a quelling motion. "This doesn't concern her."

"We worked out a thousand different angles with economics and real estate and legal, but we didn't consider this. Which is probably why our permits have been tied up in city hall for weeks now. We didn't realize the power the historical society holds—"

"Unofficial power," Christopher adds darkly.

Sutton nods. "You saw what we missed in less than a minute."

"Have you really put everything you have into this?" I know that Christopher doesn't have as much money as the trust fund. Really, who does? His was a white-collar background, for all that his mother married into my family for a few seasons. But I don't know what he has, specifically. He's always refused to take even a nominal salary for the work in managing my inheritance. Which is annoying, really. A nice salary and bonuses for the kind of growth the fund has had should be standard. Why hasn't he let me pay him for it, if he has limited funds?

"You don't need to worry about that," Christopher says, which means *yes*.

"We have enough for construction," Sutton says, "which isn't pocket change. But walking away from the library isn't really an option with what we've put into it. It's our plan A, plan B, and plan C. There's no alternative."

"Why didn't you put some of the trust fund into it? Like as an investment?"

His eyes flash. "That would be unethical."

"Like letting a sick woman suffer because you're a pompous asshole?" He could learn a thing or two about concern for your fellow human beings. He doesn't care about my mother. And he definitely doesn't care about me. *Unethical.* Ha!

"She's not suffering. Her pain is manageable and her prognosis favorable."

Surprise locks my muscles tight. There's a healthy dose of suspicion along with it. "Favorable. That's what her doctor told me last week.

Now I want to know how the hell you know anything about her condition."

"It's part of my role as executor to make sure you're safe."

That makes me laugh. Safe, because he wants nothing more than to ride in on his damned white horse. He wants to spy on us and then call it protection. "If my mother isn't allowed a single cent from the trust fund, then she's not part of your stupid role. You don't get to have it both ways."

I turn my back on him to face Sutton, who I'm finding infinitely more reasonable to deal with. The fire burnishes his golden hair, making it seem as if he's glowing. While Christopher is vibrating with tension and I'm flushed with frustration, he looks merely thoughtful. Those brilliant blue eyes sift through the things we're saying… and the things we're not saying.

"I hate to break it to you," I tell him, "but I'm not exactly rooting for your success here. So I'm probably not the best person to help with your diplomacy problem."

Sutton seems at ease in the tux and the Queen Anne chair and the stuffy old country club. It's the kind of assurance that comes from being fully comfortable with who you are. He's ambitious, but in a different way from Christopher, without the desperate, dangerous edge. His is a pure manifestation of hard work and hard play.

He's probably good with rope. The words come back to me at this completely inappropriate moment, making my cheeks heat. I have no interest in being tied up, but there's something about a man so intensely physical that draws me like a magnet.

Sutton leans forward and clasps his hands together, elbows on his knees. His eyes are sharp and as wide-open as a summer sky. "We put everything into this project because we can make even more back. This will change the city. You smooth this over for us, and we'll buy a whole damn hospital wing."

"How is that any different than Christopher giving his personal credit card?"

"Because this isn't personal. It's business."

The room feels alive with sexual tension and dark undercurrents. This is intensely personal, but he's also right in a way. It's also business—and if I earn that money through my own work, then it's fair game. As fair as any painting I've sold. "Seriously, though. You weren't even going to call the historical society?"

"And do what?" Christopher asks. "Throw a

tea party?"

"As you can see, we need your help," Sutton says, his expression sardonic.

In that moment I know I'll be spending some time in Tanglewood. Not only because it will help my mother. Despite what I said before, I do actually care about the company's success. Christopher and I have too much history for me to be apathetic, no matter how much I want to be.

He could have learned every number in the textbooks at Emerson, but they didn't prepare him to face off with the righteous Mrs. Rose-monts of the world.

And it turns out that Sutton is good with rope, at least in an abstract sense. With every word he pulls the knots a little tighter. He tugs me a little closer. I'm not sure how I let him ensnare me this way, but already it's hard to see my way free.

CHAPTER SEVENTEEN
Basically Poison

"**W**HEN ARE YOU coming home?" Mom says after picking up the phone.

I cringe a little at the word *home*, but I'm careful not to let my feelings enter my voice. She has more things to worry about than whether her daughter, fresh out of college, wants to live in the spare bedroom. So much has changed in the four years since the will reading, but in other ways everything is the same. "It'll take longer than I thought."

She sighs. "Christopher isn't going to bend, baby."

"He might," I say, because there's no point in explaining the whole thing about the library. It will only stress her out. "Actually he's being more reasonable. I think if I stay a couple more weeks, we might have it worked out."

"I don't need the experimental treatment," she says for the millionth time. "I don't want that. I only agreed because you were so adamant. My herbalist has a whole plan laid out for me, to make sure I stay in remission."

"Mom, you know what the doctor said. A good diet can help you stay strong and healthy, but it's not going to keep the cancer from coming back."

"I'm convinced it was all that coffee I drank. I never realized how toxic that stuff is. You aren't still drinking lattes, are you? It's basically poison."

I don't bother arguing with her, because the poison that caused her cancer changes every week. It was whatever they put in the facials or the chlorine in the gym's pool. I think in a weird way it helps her feel in control of what's happening to her body, being able to place the blame on something specific.

"No lattes," I say, ignoring the empty coffee cups strewn around the hotel room.

"Good. I never want you to go through this."

Worry is a hand around my chest, because mostly Mom doesn't complain about how she's feeling. She tuts and fusses and worries but she never just yells, *this fucking hurts.* I wish she would actually; it seems like that would be cathartic. This is the way she tries to help me, but the doctor was very clear on her chances for staying in remission. Which are high.

"I actually need you to do me a favor," I tell her, feeling guilty that I need this from her. There's only so many times I can wear paint-splattered clothes to the office. "Can you throw some clothes in a box and overnight them to me? I didn't pack enough."

"Oh," she says, sounding relieved. She likes it when I need her. "I can do that. What do you need, more jeans? A few bras."

"Nicer things, if you can find them. Some evening clothes. And there's this black skirt somewhere in the back. No pressure, don't spend too much energy on it, okay?"

"Evening clothes," she says, proving her mind is just as sharp as ever even if her body has wasted away to half its size. She's always been fashionably slender, but now she's painfully skinny. "What are you doing with Christopher that you need evening clothes?"

"I'm visiting Bea tomorrow night," I say, glad to have some excuse. "You remember her? Beatrix Cartwright. The daughter of the famous concert pianist."

"Of course I remember her," Mom says. "I'll send you a few cute dresses to pick from. But Harper, remember to be careful."

"Beatrix doesn't bite."

"That's not what I mean. Men like Christopher, they can be charming when they want to be."

"Don't worry, Mom. He doesn't want to be."

Which is probably the only reason I'm safe. In a weird way I'm almost grateful he's such a pompous asshole. It would be so easy to fall for him again if he weren't.

CHAPTER EIGHTEEN

Penthouse

BEATRIX CARTWRIGHT LIVES in the penthouse of L'Etoile. We met a long time ago at some party where my pink tulle itched me like crazy and the children mostly tried to stay out of sight so we didn't get roped into reciting our life goals. Then tragedy had fallen on her family, leaving her orphaned and absent from elite society.

I found her years later on the online artist scene, where I recognized her voice and her hands and her inimitable talent with the piano. Despite her large platform and success, she had managed to stay anonymous—something that made me green with envy. There were memes about my untouchable fortune that I ended up tagged on with unnerving regularity. The Internet has a long memory.

She's since gone public and found true love in the strangest place. I'm a fan of her boyfriend, Hugo Bellmont, even though he was a high-priced escort when they met. Or maybe because of that.

He's the one who meets me when I arrive, devastating in his handsomeness, his hair in perfect disarray. It feels perfectly natural that he should kiss me on both cheeks and take my wine offering with a groan that sounds sexual. "Chateau Leoville," he reads. "Nineteen eighty-nine. *Merci infiniment.* I love a great Bordeaux."

I breathe deep, taking in the scent of spices. "It smells delicious, and I haven't eaten all day. Don't tell me Bea has taken up cooking?"

"Sometimes she helps me with the vegetables, where her fingers are as efficient with a knife as they are with the piano keys, but today she has been shut into her music room."

"A difficult piece?"

"She plays it perfectly, again and again. It is the artist temperament," he says, teasing because he knows I paint. "Never satisfied."

I stick out my tongue, which only makes him laugh. "Let's call the temperamental artist to the table, because I'm ready to eat."

"Oh, but we're waiting for one more guest."

"Really," I say, flopping onto the antique couch with its bits of fluff peeking out. The penthouse is a curious mix of the old world and the new, much like the couple who inhabits it. Though Bea makes limited appearances in Tanglewood since they got together, they're both very private. I'm curious who else has made their way into the inner circle.

"It's an old friend," Hugo says as he stirs some kind of soup on the small freestanding stove. He sounds almost embarrassed, as if he should not have any friends. Or maybe not any old ones.

"From Morocco?" I ask, knowing he was born there.

"*Non,* he came to Tanglewood around the same time I did. We shared a one-bedroom apartment before either of us could afford anything more."

I refrain from asking whether this man also worked as a professional escort, but only barely. Maybe he still does that job. I could be persuaded to hire a ridiculously handsome man with nimble hands and an expressive mouth. Knowing Christopher would see the charge is a bonus.

"You will be disappointed," Hugo says, sounding rueful.

"Can you always read women's minds?"

HE DIPS A fresh spoon into the sauce and tastes it. "Ah, that's perfect. Salt and pepper and enough heat that it feels warm going down. And in answer to your question, usually."

"That must have come in handy."

"It is…" He searches for a word, looking perplexed. "A curse."

I have to laugh. "It's a great loss to the female kind that you're now monogamous."

A small bell rings near the elevator, which I assume means someone is coming up. "Well, perhaps you will not be disappointed. Sometimes you remind me of my old friend. It is the way you both seem to be more alive than the average person, more… feeling."

"That's also a curse," I say, a little wry.

The elevator door opens, and none other than Sutton Mayfair walks in. His shirtsleeves are rolled up, his slacks a little rumpled. He clearly has spent a long day at work, maybe solved a great many problems related to economics and real estate and law. From my perch on the sofa I can watch him without him noticing me, not at first.

Hugo greets him with one of those manly back slaps and a French expletive. "A nineteen eighty-five Chablis? It's truly indecent the volume of great wine we'll enjoy tonight."

Sutton takes a few steps into the penthouse and freezes. His expression is blank, which must be what surprise looks like on him. There's no indication whether he's happy to see me or whether he wishes he'd never come. No indication whether he likes this white gauzy evening gown, which was included with a few other dresses in the box that Avery sent.

She's thorough, that girl.

I would have said I had no desire to see either Sutton or Christopher so soon after our country club confrontation, but I can't deny the beat of pleasure in my veins. Colors seem more vibrant when Sutton's in the room. The strains of piano through the door more bittersweet. This must be what Hugo meant, that he's more alive than everyone else. More feeling.

"Harper," he says, cautious the way he might be around an animal. Careful not to spook me. Do I seem so wild to him? There's definitely something inside me that wants to be soothed by his large hands. It's too dangerous, though. He's too close to Christopher to be safe.

"You already know each other?" Hugo asks. "This is fortunate, then."

"Fortunate," I agree, though my voice is faint.

"She's going to be working with us on the Tanglewood Library restoration."

"I thought it was going to be more of a

teardown and rebuild?"

"She's changing that," Sutton says, his voice warm with approval. And gratitude? Somehow I've gone from being the troublemaker to the guardian angel. "We'll need the buy-in of the upper crust if we want to gentrify the west side."

That snaps me out of my Southern-drawl-induced haze. "The west side? I haven't spent a long time in Tanglewood, but isn't that a really dangerous part of town?"

"You won't be going there unescorted," Sutton says.

Even though I have no desire to stroll through dark back alleys, I don't want Sutton to worry about protecting me. It's too close to what Christopher has done. "I can take care of myself."

Sutton advances toward me, making my stomach clench. He leans over me, resting one hand on the back of the sofa. He's not touching me, not anywhere, but I can feel the heat of him. I can scent the male essence of him. It's an intimate position, his body hovering over mine.

"Don't mistake me for him," Sutton says, his voice low.

"Then don't act like him. No one has to save me."

"Save you? No, sugar. I want to peel that sexy

little dress away from your body and make love to you so hard and so long you're going to beg. You can't take anymore, that's what you'll say, and if I were a better man, one who wanted to protect you and keep you in a safe little box, I would stop. Except I won't be done with you for a long time."

A sound escapes me. It should be a protest, an outrage, but instead it's a moan. God, he's making me want this. "You're making Hugo uncomfortable."

Sutton gives a rough laugh. "He's pretending he can't see anything except his fancy French sauce, but if he thought you didn't want me, he'd have already given me a black eye. And I'd have deserved it. Do you know why he hasn't done that?"

Because he always knows what women want. It really is a curse.

I'm tired of having Sutton pursue, not because I don't want this, but because I do. Why am I holding myself back from him on account of Christopher? It's in this moment that I can admit that I still want him. Still love him. That's the only reason I could be thinking about him when another man stands right in front of me. It hurts to admit that, even privately. My fortress of protection against men and their transience, torn down in an instant of self awareness.

The heart is fickle. It doesn't listen to reason.

But I don't have to obey my heart when I know it's wrong. There's no loyalty I owe Christopher Bardot, and none he would want from me anyway.

I grasp the red silk tie in my hand and pull. A grunt of surprise, and then he's falling forward. His lips meet mine without any semblance of softness. We're all determination in this moment, which is more potent than a thousand sweet caresses. More real than a hundred whispered promises.

He deepens the kiss with one arm beneath my head, his other hand against my cheek, angling my mouth to take him better. It's consuming, this kiss... and public.

A polite cough sounds from a few yards away.

Distantly I realize the music has stopped. It's almost painful to tear my gaze away from the burning blue eyes staring down at me, made hazy and harsh with desire.

Bea stands just outside her music room, looking scandalized. "We really need to have more dinner parties, Hugo."

He crosses the room and greets her with a kiss. "Do you have a bit of the voyeur? They do make a beautiful couple."

"We're not a couple," I say quickly, but the objection loses some of the steam considering Sutton is still half over me, my leg draped over his from where I had pulled him close. Roughly I push him away and sit up, shame making my cheeks warm. "I just work for him."

"But of course," Hugo says agreeably. "That's how Bea and I met as well."

Chapter Nineteen
Goodnight Kiss

WITH ANY OTHER couple I probably would have died of embarrassment, but Hugo and Bea have a way of putting me at ease. They share a few funny stories about their cooking mishaps. There are a stack of cookbooks from around the world on a tall shelf. Mostly Hugo is a brilliant cook, but when he encounters an ingredient that's hard to get, he improvises with mixed results.

"Did you cook for Sutton when you were roommates?" Bea asks.

"I made many packages of cheap noodles."

Sutton smiles, looking a little distracted. "They were all we could afford at the time, but Hugo used to talk about food. About caviar and foie gras and other shit I'd never even tried back then."

"And what do you think now?" I ask, twirling the wineglass. A few pours of that Bordeaux, and I'm feeling downright pleased with my short public performance.

Sutton's blue gaze meets mine. "I'm a simple man."

"You know," I say, drawing a little circle on the marble table, "I'm pretty sure that's not true."

Hugo laughs. "She has you figured out."

"Not all the way," I admit. I'm a little tipsy after helping finish two bottles of wine. Not drunk. Enough to lower my guard, that's all. "Enough to know that good-old-boy act hides a lot underneath. Tell me something about you that I don't already know. No, that's too easy. Tell us something that Hugo doesn't know about you."

Sutton looks away, a half smile on his face. Not quite refusing. "And what will I get in return?"

"You're always looking to make a deal."

"That much is true. So what are you going to give me, in exchange for this secret you want?"

"What do you want?" The question comes out more seductive than I meant it to, my voice low and thick with desire. He turns me into some other woman, one who doesn't need to be rescued. One who rescues a man instead.

"A goodnight kiss," he says in that way that sounds simple but isn't.

"Only a kiss?"

He smiles. "Only that."

"Then you have yourself a deal."

"Aren't you going to shake on it?" Bea asks, her cheeks pink even though she's the only one of us who didn't touch the Bordeaux, her green eyes bright with mischief. "If the deal's going to be official, you should shake hands."

Sutton appears solemn as he offers his hand over the table, on top of the empty platter of coq au vin and the brandy-sauce green beans. I grasp the warm strength of him, the rough calluses of him, and squeeze. He gives a gentle squeeze in return. Our bodies can speak a language more fluently than our mouths, communicating, negotiating.

"A good secret," I warn him, "or the deal is off."

He considers the final swallow of red wine in his glass, taking his time to come up with what he's going to share. "There was a horse named Cinnamon," he finally says.

"That's your secret?" I mean, it's an adorable secret. But it's not enough. "I'm going to blow you a kiss. That's all you're getting for that secret."

He holds up a finger, and I realize he's tipsy too. "That's not the end of it. Giving her a name was more wishful thinking. She was wild, that one. Unbreakable. My dad kept her because she was a beauty, hoping one day they'd tame her. But really it was shitty to keep her locked up when she wouldn't let anyone near her. And then one day I went out to the stable, and she was gone. I checked everywhere—the whole stable and the pastures, but the latch had been moved from the outside, so she couldn't have gotten out alone."

This suddenly strikes me as a tragedy, and I realize I should have been more specific. A funny secret. The kind that will make us laugh. Instead something terrible is going to happen.

"Finally found her down by the lake, where the kid who worked as a farmhand in the summer was trying to coax her to keep going. She wasn't budging."

"He was running away," I whisper, recognizing the ache in my chest.

There had been an unfortunate number of times I contemplated that action, not because the streets of LA would have been hospitable but out of pure desperation. But I worried about who would take care of my mother if I left. She would have blamed herself.

Daddy would have blamed her, too.

"His home life was pretty shit. Everyone knew

that. Daddy drank too much. Mom worked to pay rent and to stay out of the way. He showed up with bruises that people pretended not to see. But he rode Cinnamon when no one else could go near her. Rode her bareback without getting thrown off and breaking his neck. If the beast weren't nervous about crossing the stream at the border of the land, if he hadn't been worried she'd break her leg, he would have been halfway across the county with her."

"What happened?" Bea asked, looking sick with worry.

Hugo touches her hand, a caress that speaks volumes. "Do not worry. Even Sutton is not so careless that he would tell a tragedy over dinner conversation."

Then he gives Sutton a look that promises stark retribution if Sutton had really been so careless.

Sutton grins. "Where I'm from, we had more tragedy than comedy. But this story does have a happy ending. I brought the boy and the horse back home, and my dad moved him up from shoveling hay to working with the horses. He tamed Cinnamon before he grew up and left."

There are tears in Bea's eyes. "That's the saddest thing I've ever heard."

Hugo makes a clucking sound before pulling her into his arms, onto his lap, uncaring that he has an audience. I could paint them this way, the handsome charmer and the old-world beauty, both of them made hard by the world and soft again for each other.

And then something clicks. "Oh my God."

"You see it?" Sutton asks, his voice low. "I thought it would just be me, pretending not to."

"What are you talking about?" Hugo says, a notch between his brows. "Ma belle, are you ill?"

"No, but she does have a condition," I say, trying to contain my excitement and failing. "Bea, why didn't you tell me? I hate you! Okay, I'm over it. I love you again. This is so exciting!"

There are many expressions Hugo can wear comfortably—amusement and sarcasm and seduction. I've never seen this one. Astonishment. "What?"

Bea's cheeks are more than pink now. They're a deep peach, so dark they match her freckles. "I wasn't sure how you'd react," she says a little shyly. "We didn't talk about children."

Hugo's mouth remains open. He looks shocked beyond words.

"Not a sip of wine all evening," Sutton says in that drawl. "Even though I brought the Chablis because she loves it."

"And she got emotional over the horse story," I add. "Really, for someone who is famous for being able to read women, you completely missed this one."

"We never have perspective about the people closest to us," Sutton says, watching the embracing couple with satisfaction.

Hugo murmurs in French, sounding breathless and adrift. "*Un enfant?*"

"Are you angry?" Bea whispers.

She might be worried, but I can already see the stirrings of hope inside him. They may not have talked about children, but Hugo is committed to her fully. And a family is exactly what he needs to feel grounded in this life. He kisses her with a passion so raw and charmless it looks like a different man, one without an ounce of finesse. There's only love.

"We should go," I whisper to Sutton, who has already pushed back his chair. We make our exit with discreet haste, not a second too soon judging from the way dishes crash as the two move their passion to the top of the dining table.

I'm laughing with breathless anticipation as I collapse against the mirrored walls of the elevator. "She's going to have a baby! Oh my God, we should make them name it Harper if it's a girl or Sutton if it's a boy. We were there when she told him."

He does this silent huff of amusement. "Sutton is too rough of a name for any child of theirs. Maybe they can name him Harper, even if it's a boy. It works for both."

"I like that plan," I say, grinning because I can't seem to stop. I blame the wine that I was forced to drink since Bea didn't have any tonight. My heart beats fast and light, effervescent as a Chardonnay.

The elevator opens to the bottom floor, and I step out—my smile giving way to nerves. There are a hundred people milling around the lobby, but I might as well be alone with Sutton. The way he looks at me, it's like I'm the only woman in the hotel.

A couple in a hurry jostle me, and Sutton moves to block me with his body. It's only a small pain, the bustle from a crowd, but he takes it from me. There's a gentleman underneath all that laconic Southern charm, but it's different from Christopher. He doesn't claim to know better than me. He only wants to shield me from any pain. In some ways it's a subtle distinction, but in another way they're worlds apart.

"Invite me upstairs," Sutton says, his voice low and private.

"I don't think that's a good idea." The words come out unsteady, my body humming with anticipation as if I've already agreed to whatever happens next.

"A goodnight kiss," he says. "That was the deal."

My lips feel ultrasensitive, even thinking about kissing him. "You didn't really finish the story. We were interrupted."

"That's why you're going to invite me to your room. Where it's private."

A catch in my breath. "You're very sure of yourself."

He leans close, pressing me into a corner behind the penthouse's private elevator. The only people near us are passing by, on their way to a restaurant or a theater. "I've been poor longer than I've been rich, but you know one thing that stays the same?"

Sex, my mind supplies helpfully. *Sex is the same.* "No."

"People underestimate you because you're different, that's what stays the same. The way you looked at me and heard my accent and figured you could use me to get to Christopher."

"I d-didn't think—"

"Now look at you, so close there's only linen and silk between us, your cheeks all rosy, your eyes wide. You would let me do anything to you with people a few feet away, but I'm not going to touch you."

A sense of loss rushes through me, like a hollow opened up beneath an ocean. I may not have thought I was underestimating him, but clearly I had. "Come upstairs."

Blue eyes flash with triumph. "Lead the way."

Lead the way, because this is under my control. It's up to me whether Sutton comes upstairs to my room, whether I use the key card to let us both inside, whether he wakes beside me in the morning. How would his body look, sated and tangled in white rumpled sheets? His skin would be leather-rough everywhere, exposed to the elements from a young age.

Or would he still be velvet and smooth in some places?

We take a regular elevator up to my floor, both of us silent in front of an older couple returning after an early night. The only place we touch is his palm at the small of my back—such an innocent place, that. There shouldn't be a fire burning, spreading outward, down to my ass and between my legs. His gentle pressure shouldn't make me think of other ways he could hold me.

Even when the older couple steps out, we don't move from our assigned spots. My feet have become part of the floor, too heavy to move. He's immobile beside me.

The dial that tells us which floor we're on is made of a brass arrow and roman numerals. Nothing so coarse as a digital screen could grace this elevator. A low bell signals that we've arrived. The doors slide open.

It's someone else walking out of the elevator with a warm hand at her back, another body that manages to put one foot in front of the other in high heels.

A baroque mirror hanging on the wall shows a pretty woman beside a man twice her size, his face set in stern lines. They look well matched in an unexpected way, small against his strength, delicate where he's broad. *People underestimate you because you're different.* He's right about one thing. We aren't the same. We're two different elements: water and stone.

At the end of the hallway we come to my room. It's cowardice that turns my face down so I can fumble blindly through my small clutch. There are twenty million cards in here, none of them the hotel room key. I'm running out of breath even though I'm standing still.

A hand covers mine, and I freeze. How is he so calm at a moment like this? Has he been to a thousand hotel rooms with a thousand other desperate heiresses?

There are small white marks and raised lines. "Scars?" I whisper.

He knows what I mean. "Sometimes knives. Or barbed wire. A few wild animals have got their teeth in me over the years."

"Is that a euphemism?" I still can't bring myself to look him in the eye.

Especially when he laughs, low and rough. "Suppose so. You want to take a piece out of me, Harper St. Claire? I think you just might before you're done."

Then I do meet that blue gaze, because he has it wrong. "It's the other way around. I don't do... this. Whatever this is. I'm out of my depth here."

It's like ripping myself open, being so vulnerable with a man. I learned not to trust them early, from the men my mom married, from my father. Sutton could use this knowledge against me.

Those eyes turn dark with tenderness. And this, I realize, is what makes him different. This is the way that I underestimated him. Where he could have been cold and unfeeling, there's this humanity to him instead. Humanity, but also pure male desire.

"We'll start slow," he says, and then his hand holds my face.

"Why me?" I've been pursued by men before, but never like this. "Is this some kind of competition thing? Because of my connection to Christopher?"

He gives a rough laugh. "Jesus Christ. You're beautiful, smart, funny. Your connection to Christopher is the *least* interesting thing about you. I don't give a damn who your stepbrother is."

"I have to tell you something—" The words catch in my throat. "I think... what I mean to say is... I'm a little hung up on Christopher. I don't want to be. I didn't even think I was, but sitting there with you and Hugo and Bea, I realized it's true."

He's laughing, the bastard, a silent, shaking kind of laugh. "Do you think that's a surprise to me?"

I scrunch my nose. "It's a surprise to me."

"For your information I knew it as soon as you walked into the boardroom. It was clear from the way you talked about him, but it wasn't going to stop me. Do you know why?"

"Because you want to have sex with me."

A slow shake of his head. "I want to have sex with you so bad it hurts. It's a distraction, the way my cock gets hard every time I look at you. The way I can't stop imagining your breasts under those little T-shirts you wear. And that dress at the gala. It took every ounce of strength in me not to rip it apart with my bare hands, the Tangle-wood Historical Society be damned."

My breath catches. "A distraction."

"A distraction, because I'm not only trying to have sex with you. I'm a direct man, honey. And I'm going to be direct about this. I'm courting you."

"Courting?" My voice sounds faint. What an old-fashioned word. A lovely word. God, it's a terrifying word.

"That's what a man does when he's determined and serious and wants a woman for his own. So yeah, you're hung up on another man. You work on that little distraction while I work on one of my own."

That's the only warning I get before his lips cover mine. There are seconds that I could use to protest. *No, I'm not ready, wait.* My mouth stubbornly silent until he finds it.

I gasp my surprise, but he swallows that down.

It feels good to be wanted, uninhibited, without a million reasons why we can't be together. Without that unbreakable control that makes Christopher Bardot a man without weakness.

Of course I can't deny that he's part of this equation. He's Sutton's business partner. He'll find out what we did, eventually. Will he feel regret? Jealousy? I hope so. Maybe that's small of me, but there's a much bigger part of me that wants him to finally, *finally* notice me.

Whatever I give Sutton he takes, even the trembling almost-kiss that seems to be all I can manage. If he really has been with a thousand other heiresses, they must know how to kiss better than this. I'm all rapid heartbeat and heavy breaths and sharp little whimpers.

He doesn't seem to mind, shifting so his body is closer to mine, a steady presence that manages to soothe me. My back hits the wall of the hotel, and in the cool surface I can make out the gentle embossing of fleurs-de-lis. I'm the princess and the pea, my heated skin sensing even the slightest bump beneath layers of cloth. Who knew she was just turned on?

His hands are on my waist, and I have to

move my body, have to gasp against his mouth, hoping he'll understand. There's an ache at my breast, and the only thing that will fix it is his touch. He takes the permission with a groan of surrender, cupping me through the filmy fabric of my dress.

On his tongue I taste the wine and the chocolate we had for dessert. I taste the man underneath, something elemental and addictive.

My mind is cloudy with the sensation of him, his touch and his taste. His rough breathing, the proof that I'm affecting this powerful man as much as he's affecting me. I tug at his clothes, yanking at his shirt as if I can tear it away from his flesh.

"Slow," he murmurs, his voice rough. "Steady with you."

Like I'm a horse. The thought makes me laugh, though it's a little wild. He swallows the laugh, too, drinking me down like he's been dying of thirst. This stops being about Christopher Bardot and my revenge against his control. It starts being about the very male, very aroused body pressing against me, and all the elemental ways he wakes me up inside.

His thumb sweeps over the curve of my breast, searching, soothing, until my nipple becomes hard. And still he moves his thumb, back and forth, driving me insane. I make little whimpers because I can't do anything else; we could have done this downstairs. He's right. It's terrible, but he's right. I would have let him do anything, everything, if only it will calm this ache.

"Please," I say, panting, pulling at the buttons on his shirt. "Come inside."

He sinks his teeth into the flesh of my bottom lip, like a punishment, and I yelp because it only hurts when he pulls away. His eyes are a deep ocean blue, at the very bottom of the earth. "Are you sure?"

"Yes," I say, but it's really a hiss in the quiet hum of the hallway.

"Because we don't have to—"

"Oh my God, if you say that you know better than me, I'm going… I'm going to… I don't even know what I'll do, but it's definitely not have sex with you."

My head falls to the side, because I'm fed up with men who tell me what to do, fed up with myself, because I keep falling for them, and that's when I see his hand in a fist against the wall. All that frustration pressed against the pretty wallpaper, because he doesn't want to rush me.

It warms me enough that it's a surprise when

his mouth nips my throat, making me jump. He nips me again, a little lower this time. And then moves the edge of his teeth along my collarbone. There's something primal about him. Something dangerous and possessive, but he doesn't use his power to control me. He kisses me lower, between my breasts—and then even lower, on my stomach through the dress. That's when I realize he's on his knees.

Somewhere between the kissing and now, this man sank to his knees. He's on the threadbare carpet, looking up at me. It's like having a wild animal bow to you in the jungle. I'm panting, afraid to move.

"What are you doing?" I whisper, even though I want to say, *Don't stop, don't stop.*

"The goodnight kiss."

"We already did that." My lips feel swollen from what he did to me. It was more than a kiss, more than a claiming. He changed the molecules that form me, made me crave him. An ordinary peck will never be enough after this. Not when I know what's possible.

He shakes his head, slow and determined. "Not yet."

Without breaking eye contact he reaches down to the hem of my dress, pulling and pulling the fabric, revealing inches of my bare leg. It's indecent, what's happening in this hallway. At the very least we should be inside the room for this, but I can't bring myself to stop him.

The dress is held up in bunches, the delicate silk spilling from between blunt fingers. I know the exact moment when he sees what I'm wearing underneath—the sharp intake of breath. There weren't any panties in my carry-on bag to wear with this dress.

I only packed boring, utilitarian things to wear when confronting Christopher Bardot about my mother's hospital bill. There was no way I could have guessed that I would end up backed up against a wall by this man, my dress ruched up to my waist, exposing my bare pussy to the world— or at least anyone on this floor who decides to open their door.

They would be shocked to see me, not only my bare sex. They would be shocked to see the way my upper body leans against the wall, needing its support, one shoulder strap of my dress fallen loose, my eyes heavy-lidded with acquiescence to whatever happens next. There's a sense that I've done more than submit to him; that I've ordered him to his knees. Not with words but by need. Everything about his broad shoulders and his hard features speak of power, and it's an unspeakable thrill to realize that he bows to me.

God, what power a woman can wield.

One hand holds my skirts while the other runs up the outside of my calf. The inside of my thigh. His knuckles brush my sex, and I let my legs fall open. "Please, I need—"

"I know what you need." His voice is like the rush of wind between two mountains, something that my body recognizes as eternal, that he was here before me.

That he'll be here when I'm gone.

His fingers touch me with agonizing lightness, exploring, teasing. Letting me remain open for discovery. Is that part of what makes this hotter, knowing anyone might walk in on us? He has unending patience, even though I can see his arousal in the line of his suit pants where he kneels. I can see the arousal in the haze in his blue eyes, in the hard set of his jaw.

He's like Atlas, cursed to carry the weight of the world. Strong enough to actually succeed in such an impossible task. Of course that makes me the world—and that's how it feels, when he leans forward to place a chaste kiss on my thigh.

Higher, higher. He likes to tease me. There's

something playful about him that's at odds with the burden he carries. Even the gods know how to make light of themselves.

And then he kisses my clit, and I lose the ability to think. My shoulders press into the wall. My hips push out toward his mouth. There's nothing but his mouth and the magical things he can do with it. I cry out, and the sound of it echoes back to me in the empty hallway.

Even in this he has that terrible patience. That terrible playfulness that lets him nip at my skin, lets him tug and tease me until I'm shameless—pressing myself against his mouth, his nose, his chin, desperate for that friction my body demands.

His laugh surrounds me, piercing the madness that consumes me. "I should leave you like this," he says, murmuring almost to himself. "You'd fuck yourself against the bedpost all night long, but it wouldn't be the same. Wouldn't be enough."

"You wouldn't," I say on an aching gasp. "I'm dying here."

He looks up at me, and it's strange that he does have sympathy for me. It's there in his blue eyes even while his lips shine with my arousal. "Are you?" he asks, his voice not shaking one little bit. Not like mine. "Or I could lay you down on the bed and tie you there, so you couldn't get off. You'd keep trying all night, this gorgeous body fucking the air, desperate for relief. I could watch you all night."

"Nooo," I say, pushing my hips toward him as if that might convince him.

I'm beyond logic right now. Beyond anything but pure undiluted begging. I've never been more desperate than in this moment; this is what he's reduced me to. This is what he holds in his hands.

"Whatever you want."

And the bastard, he sits back on his heels. His hands fall to his side, somehow more powerful that way, his head looking up at me. He commands this hallway. This hotel. He commands the whole world from his goddamn knees. "Now you're ready to make a deal."

"Ruthless." The word spills from my lips before I've thought it through. I've known so many men who were ruthless, including Christopher, but never one who's managed to disarm me as much as Sutton Mayfair. That makes him infinitely more dangerous.

Casually he trails two fingers up my calf and back down. "Yes."

"Because you've been poor longer than you've

been rich." It's made him hungry, and I can't really blame him for that. I've known what it was like to be poor, painfully poor, in small, infinitesimal drips. In the space between my mother's husbands.

"That," he says, with a faint dip of his head. "And because I don't underestimate you, Harper."

I swallow hard, because I've been underestimated all my life. Is that why he told me the story about the little boy who everyone underestimated? Suddenly that strikes me as totally unfair. "You didn't tell a secret about you. You told me a secret about a wild horse."

A faint smile. "The secret is that I wasn't the boy with a family and a ranch. I was the one who showed up with bruises. I was the one who tamed Cinnamon."

"No," I whisper.

"I told you, Harper. The story had a happy ending."

Touching him is as natural as breathing, as inevitable as the ache in my chest. Bristles on his jaw brush my palm. "I wish that hadn't happened to you."

"Maybe the moral of the story is that I can tame wild animals." He's a little mocking, making fun of himself. I'm the one worried that it might be true.

I snatch my hand away. It would be a lie to say I'm not a wild animal, since I'm considering scratching him in response to the ownership in his blue eyes. "I'm not tame."

There it is again, that warm persistence that has made him rich when he was poor. It earned him enough money and know-how to partner with Christopher, a man who, for all his many faults, is admittedly a business genius. *Not yet,* he seems to say without words.

And I'm not entirely sure he's wrong.

The elevator down the hall dings, and in a startled rush I push down my skirt. I expect to see the disgruntled businessman who's staying in the room beside me or one of the other occupants I haven't passed yet.

Instead Christopher Bardot steps off the elevator, his dark eyes narrowing on mine immediately, emotions flashing across his face before he manages to put a cold mask over them all. But I saw them. For that brief second I saw jealousy and anger, and something that breaks my heart—hurt.

In front of me Sutton moves much more slowly, getting up as casually as if he had been sitting at dinner, taking the time to straighten his shirt.

Then, impossibly, he runs a thumb across his bottom lip. And presses it between his lips to savor the taste of it. Of me. It's the most explicit thing I've ever seen in my life, and we're both fully clothed and covered.

Christopher's eyes flash. "What the hell are you doing here?"

I'm not the kind of girl that men fight over, am I? I didn't think so, but there's leashed violence simmering in the air.

"Do you need it spelled out?" Sutton asks in that drawl I'm coming to realize is a sign of danger. The kind of danger that most people don't expect from a Southern boy.

"What are *you* doing here?" I demand, because we're in front of my hotel room. And what the hell does Christopher think, showing up here at night? Embarrassment threatens to strangle me, but I remind myself firmly that I'm a grown woman. I have every right to do what I want... even though I possibly should have been inside the hotel room.

It's a question of a few feet, so I hold my chin up.

"I came to talk to you," Christopher says in a low voice.

There's a small move, barely discernible, the

way that Sutton moves to block me. As if protecting me from Christopher. "You can talk tomorrow. At the office."

"This is personal," Christopher says, his eyes locked on mine.

He's waiting for me to send Sutton away, except I'm not sure that's what I should do.

If that kiss had been only for revenge, only to crack Christopher's cool veneer, then it already succeeded. But Sutton made it more than that. He made it about me and him, when I didn't think it was possible for me to desire another man.

"There's nothing personal between us. You made sure of that. There's only money between us."

For all his rough background, Sutton wouldn't do anything as uncouth as gloat. He doesn't say a word or even move a muscle. He's a monolith, but a sense of victory rises around him—unmistakable. I may as well have written his name on my body with permanent marker; that's the way these men are taking my declaration.

Is that how I mean it? I don't belong to Sutton, but God, I was never Christopher's. Even in my teenage fantasies I should have known better than to hope for that.

"She's my sister," Christopher says.

A harsh laugh. "That would be more convincing if I didn't think you were going to beat off to the image of her leaning against the wall, looking fucked out and hot as all hell."

"Jesus," Christopher says, baring his teeth to Sutton in a sign of frustration. "How dare you make this a competition? How dare you use her to get to me?"

The words find their mark inside my heart, sharp and poisoned. I don't want to be a ball that men throw around for sport. A toy to be put aside when they get bored of me.

Where there had been victory, now there is only menace. How does Sutton manage to exude feelings without moving a muscle? His energy shimmers around him, thick in the air. And now he's pissed. "How dare you imply that's the only reason a man would want her?"

All the heat that had been burning through my body leaks into the walls and warms the floors. None of it's left inside my body. I'm cold. "Is this a game to you?"

I don't even know who I'm asking. Probably Sutton. I already know what Christopher wants from me, and it's to save me from myself. Not exactly a flattering sentiment, but a familiar one.

Sutton turns to me, his jaw hard. "He's going to tell you I'm a bastard." He cups my face, running his thumb along my lower lip. The same thumb that he used to touch my arousal on his lip. His head bends low so only I can hear what he says. "And he's right about that. Because a better man would leave you to him. I want you for myself." His mouth claims mine in a kiss that my body responds to even while my mind is confused. He explores me with sensual leisure, standing between Christopher and myself. There's no doubt what my body wants when I look up at him with my lips parted and my eyelids heavy.

That's how Sutton leaves me, leaning against the wall, my limbs weak and my mind hazy from wanting him—from wanting what he was going to do before Christopher interrupted us. *I could lay you down on the bed and tie you there, so you couldn't get off. You'd keep trying all night, this gorgeous body fucking the air, desperate for relief. I could watch you all night.* It's strange that he can make even torture a thing that I long for—that fact seems important. Momentous. Something about man and woman and the ways we break, but I can't think about anything but the throb between my legs. And the hard look in Christopher's eyes.

My purse must have fallen to the floor at some point. The cards are scattered across the worn carpet. And there is the hotel key card, the one I couldn't find before.

Christopher is the one who bends to pick it up, gathering the rest of the contents in a broad sweep of his strong hands. He doesn't bother handing the purse back to me, which is just as well since I don't think I could hold anything. Instead he uses the key card to open the door, and holds it open for me.

How strange, that it should feel like a betrayal for me to be with another man when Christopher has rejected me for so long. And strange that he should still be bent on being the white knight.

My mind is too muddled to solve this, so I let him usher me inside. Let him pour me a drink of water from the minibar. Let him sit me down in a chair while he stands in front of me like some kind of strict professor, his eyes intense and a muscle in his jaw ticking.

I know I should be thinking about the trust fund and hospital bills, but all I can hear is Sutton's voice saying, *You'd fuck yourself against the bedpost all night long, but it wouldn't be the same.*

Wouldn't be enough.

I'm used to the way Christopher distracts me, the way I can't seem to stop thinking about him even though I shouldn't. I'm less used to the way I can't seem to stop thinking about Sutton. What are these men doing to me? Despite all their differences, they fit together as business partners. Both of them are ruthless and so complex they're going to drive me insane.

"I know you hate me," Christopher says, and I don't bother to correct him. I'm not sure I could find the words. *I hate you so much you consume me. And now there's Sutton, doing the same thing. What will be left of me?* "And I deserve that."

"So you're going to let me pay the hospital?"

He gives me a severe look. "I'm being completely honest when I say that Sutton isn't good for you. Women love him and he loves them back... for about a week. Maybe two."

"Then this shouldn't be a problem for very long," I say, even though my insides squeeze at the thought of being pushed aside. It almost seems worth it, to experience the wild power of Sutton, even knowing that heartbreak is on the horizon.

"You should stay away from him. Go back to New York."

"Does ordering people around work well for you? Because I really want to do the opposite of whatever you say." I would have done the opposite anyway, but now I want to make a point.

He runs a hand over his face. "I'm trying to look out for you. Sutton uses people."

"You went into business with him."

Christopher holds the bedpost, a carved wooden bulb that makes me think of dirty things. Maybe I'll always look at bedposts differently now. "That's exactly why I went into business with him. Because I'm going to succeed no matter what. No matter what some society thinks about my plans."

I shake my head, remembering when I saw him in his cabin on the yacht, head bent over his textbook late at night. He's always been driven. And clueless. "You really do need me."

"I don't need anyone."

The words ring in the silence that follows, an explanation of what came before and foretelling of what happens next. It's the heart of this man, his determination not to need anyone. Even the people who love him. That's what I felt for him, once. It took me years to admit it to myself, the reason why I could never get serious with a boy after him.

"Well," I say softly. "Regardless of whether you need me, here I am. I'm going to do the job Sutton's given me, and then you're going to pay for that butterfly garden."

A notch between dark eyebrows. "Tell me why."

"That was the deal," I say, deliberately avoiding the question. It's easier to deal with Christopher when he's purely hypothetical. Harder when I place the issue in front of him. He becomes flesh and blood. Vulnerable. Fallible. I don't want him to be wrong, because I'd hate him. I don't want him to be right, because I'd have to stop hating him. And that would mean facing what he means to me, which should be nothing at all.

He growls. "You know what I mean. Why do you need to pay for a damn butterfly garden when she's in remission?"

"You must have been keeping tabs on her to know so much."

"Apparently they left something out."

His bluntness makes me laugh, though nothing is funny right now. "There's a pretty high chance that it will come back, and then we'd have to do it all again. The radiation... God, it nearly killed her on its own. She won't do it again. She already said so."

He stares for a moment. "She'll change her mind."

My stomach clenches, because that's what I want. "Contrary to what you think, people don't work like machines that do whatever you program them to do."

"She'll change her mind if it's the only way."

"You don't know her," I say sharply. "And you sure as hell don't care about her, so don't pretend to me. But there is another way. There's an experimental treatment. A study that's already full, but they're going to make an exception."

He makes a rough sound. "Oh, that's rich. Trading the chance to live for a new goddamn butterfly garden. Very noble of them."

"That's the way the world works. The only reason they even made me the offer is because they knew I could afford it. Or at least they thought I could."

Christopher turns away, looking out at the dark window. It's too reflective, showing his silhouette and my shoulders at the forefront of the city. "I didn't know."

"It doesn't change anything, though. Does it?" He's still not going to let the trust fund pay for the butterfly garden. It has nothing to do with money.

Everything to do with control.

He swings back to face me, at least doing me the courtesy of looking into my eyes when he shakes his head. "No. I can see why that made you grateful to Sutton, the offer he made, but he's doing this for our project. Or to get under your dress."

It doesn't even occur to Christopher that he's basically calling me a prostitute, suggesting that the only reason I let Sutton touch me is out of gratitude for a job. There's no anger in me, because even though Daddy made me messed up about men and money, he also helped me understand them.

"What I do with Sutton is my own business," I say, before adding, "You made sure of that when you pushed me away after the will reading."

His throat works. "I shouldn't have been so hard on you."

That makes me smile, bittersweet. There's an old thread in my chest, worn and threadbare, one I could have sworn was broken years ago. Trust for the man named Christopher Bardot, that thread. It tugs in this moment, somehow still there. "Oh sure, you should have. Your goal was to make sure no part of that stupid crush survived, and it worked."

"I do… care about you," he says in the most awkward declaration ever.

And then I have to stand up, because I'm not the woman who's going to take orders from this man. He would have to work a hell of a lot harder than that. It makes me angry to hear these things I would have swooned over four years ago. Where was he, then? It's too late now. I'm older and wiser. And a hell of a lot more guarded. "As a sister?"

He shakes his head, eyes glittering. "Never."

"As a friend?"

There's an unsteady laugh. "You were more of a friend than I deserved."

There's too much of the old Christopher in those words. Too much of the boy who looked up at the Medusa painting with awe for me to breathe easy. It makes me want to push him away.

"If you wanted to have sex with me," I say, running a finger down his white collar. "You only had to ask. When I was on the yacht. Or in front of that Medusa painting. I would have done it, Christopher. Don't you know that? I would have done anything you asked."

"Hell," he says, tight and broken.

"I think you did know, but you walked away."

He looks furious. And despairing. "It was never simple between us."

"So don't you dare show up now and tell me who I can touch. If I want to let him press me up against the wall, if he gets down on his knees and puts his mouth on me until everyone on this floor knows what we're doing, that's my business. You had your chance."

My body heats at the words, at the remembered pleasure of Sutton's mouth on my sex. Christopher looks down at me, as if he can feel the heat emanating from between my legs. His expression turns stark, as if he's in pain. That's only fair, because I'm in pain too.

"You deserve better than that," Christopher says, but there's no way to pretend he's talking about Sutton. He's talking about himself and we both know it.

"He gives me what I want, which is something you might try next time you like a girl."

"It wasn't that," he says, harsh again.

"No?" I step forward and place a hand on his chest, feeling the way his heart beats strong and fast. He may want to be unaffected by me, but he isn't. I tilt my face up toward him. "You didn't imagine me naked in the cabin later?"

He sucks in a breath. "You were too young

then."

My words come out as a whisper. "What about now? Will you do what Sutton said—imagine me in this dress when you go home after this?"

"It's not fucking decent," he says, even though the silk covers every part of me. It's a perfectly respectable dress, when it's not hitched up around my waist.

"You can thank Sutton for this," I say, because it's true. He's the only reason I lean forward and place my lips against Christopher's, touching them in some terrible attempt to show him what he gave up, to prove to myself that I don't care about either of them.

Christopher sucks in a breath. For a second I think he's going to pull away. He stiffens and grasps my hair with his fist. Easy enough for him to stop the kiss. Instead he dips my head back and deepens it, exploring my mouth with his teeth, his tongue. Opening me wider until I whimper. Pulling me close until I can feel how hard he is beneath his slacks.

His other hand fists in the gauze of my dress, and I realize he's holding me with both hands clenched—one in my hair and one in my clothes. I don't know whether he's doing it so he doesn't have to touch me or because it's a way to control me without bruising me. He uses both hands to tug me closer; I'm pressed so tightly I can't imagine getting away.

Where Sutton had been raw sensuality and playfulness, Christopher is pure determination. He kisses me like he's a conquering army, like I'm made of gold he has to grasp—or lose forever.

I push away from him with a pained cry, because I want to stay in his arms. I want to let Christopher take me to bed and show me how much he can conquer, his way made slick by my arousal for another man. "You should go."

He pants, his pupils large and dark. "Let me stay. I want to taste you."

The words are like a cold splash of water on top of my head. Taste me, like Sutton did in the hallway. Taste me after Sutton challenged him that way. Am I only a competition between two business partners, who probably compete over more than women?

This is exactly what I always wanted, having Christopher beg for a night with me. Exactly what I always dreamed, but I can't trust it. Not when I wanted him to find out about this. Maybe not by walking into the hallway, but I knew he'd eventually find out I kissed Sutton.

Some female part of me knew exactly what I was doing, even if I couldn't admit it to myself. Now it's worked, and it's a hollow victory. Like giving him a love potion and then preening when he falls for me. It isn't real. None of this is real.

"I'll see you tomorrow," I manage to say. "Bright and early. We can work like people who need money and not from a trust fund. Like people who didn't almost have sex the night before."

He flinches, which is what I wanted. For him to feel as cold as I do. "Harper."

"No," I cry, losing my tenuous grip on composure. "You had your chance with me. Now you don't want me to be with someone else?"

"It's not about that," he says, but he's a liar. Like the man on the plane with a secret girlfriend in New York all those years ago. And like Daddy.

That's what men know how to do: make money and lie to women.

"Get out," I say, turning away. I'm not even angry with Christopher. I'm mad at myself for letting him in the room. For letting Sutton walk me here. For trusting them even when I don't have any reason to. Because that's something women are good at: loving men we shouldn't.

CHAPTER TWENTY
Wake-Up Call

I OPEN MY eyes and stare at the chandelier lit by sunrise, wondering where the hell I am and why I'm awake. Then the hotel room phone rings again. Briefly I fantasize about throwing it across the room. Or maybe attempting to flush it down the toilet.

Instead I answer with a sleepy, "Hello."

"Mademoiselle St. Claire, this is your requested wake-up call," says a voice in lightly accented French. It makes me wonder if L'Etoile hired him only for that accent. They do love ambiance. "At six o'clock. Would you like us to send breakfast?"

"Coffee," I manage to croak before letting the receiver roll out of my hand. It hangs over the side of the bed, because I'm too exhausted to pick it up.

In my defense I've been a college student and an artist for the past few years. Being Instagram famous doesn't exactly require waking up early. I know without asking that the men will be awake early, regardless of what happened last night, and I'm determined to pull my weight, to actually earn the money they're damn well going to pay me.

I drag myself out of bed and into the shower, where a spray of hot water finally lures me into consciousness. While I'm inside, I hear the room service knocking.

"Coffee," I tell the shower wall, and it echoes the word back at me, sounding relieved.

I'm in my towel when I open the door.

Sutton looks ridiculously fresh and awake at this ungodly hour, his suit crisp across his broad shoulders, narrow at the waist. His only saving grace is the cup of coffee he holds, the white lid and green stirrer keeping the heat and steam inside. It's not from the hotel, this one.

"Bless you," I tell him fervently, taking the coffee and backing up.

He steps inside with a grin, with absolutely zero shame in his blue eyes as he takes in the tops of my breasts above the towel. "A very good morning."

My body responds as if he just stood up after kneeling at my feet, his hands on my thighs, his mouth on my clit. Sparks between my legs. Heat in my breasts. My nipples turning hard against thick cotton. "How did you know I'd be awake?"

"I was hoping to find you still in bed," he admits. "I would have joined you."

"You're only a few minutes late for that."

It's a struggle to take the little green stirrer out without letting the towel drop, but naturally he doesn't help me whatsoever. He's not quite a gentleman.

Not when it means he can see my skin covered in droplets.

"There's always tomorrow," he says. "I was going to drive you over to the library, so you can see what's there before I show you the plans."

The coffee burns down my throat, the perfect blend of sharp and sweet. "If you bring me coffee like this, you can take me anywhere you want."

A knock comes at the door. "Room service."

Sutton gives my body one last look, his blue eyes tinged with regret. "You should probably get dressed. I'll get the door."

It's with a sense of disappointment that I retreat to the walk-in closet, quickly dropping the towel and sorting through the clothes that are in my luggage. It would be nice to have a power suit or something equally professional, but instead I'll have to settle for a flowing sage green skirt and a white T-shirt that says, *You should see my active bitch face.*

A quick brush of powder covers some of the freckles that make me look twelve years old. And there's nothing to be done about my hair, which falls damp and sea-blown no matter what I do. There's a mirror on the door, and I look at my hazel eyes, wondering what Sutton sees in them.

Sutton uses people. That's what Christopher said, as if I didn't know what men want from women. Even if I've never had sex before, that doesn't mean I'm totally naive to their ways. I've been to plenty of frat parties. Walked in on one of my professors and his student, once.

And there was that husband of my mother's, the one who climbed into my bed.

I know what men want from women; I'm only surprised that a man like Sutton wants it from me. Does he think I have more experience than I do? It might be a disappointment when he finds out I can paint a siren better than I can be one.

Sutton reclines on the armchair in the corner, scrolling through his phone. There are probably a hundred emails in his inbox. Phone calls to return. Or maybe he's looking at his bank balance, counting the money. That seems like something an ambitious man would do.

He looks up, and nothing about his expression changes. At least not that I can discern, but there's a sense of amusement glinting in his eyes. "You are the most interesting woman I've ever met, Harper St. Claire."

"Oh good," I say, picking up the coffee he brought me. It's infinitely stronger than whatever the hotel has in that silver carafe. "I thought you wanted me to be sexy, which was nerve-racking. The interesting thing I've been doing for years."

His lips press together like he's holding something inside, which I've already figured out is an unusual look for him. He says what he's thinking.

"What?" I say, looking down at my shirt. "Too much?"

He barks a laugh. "God, woman. You'll be the death of me."

"Now you're just being cruel." I grab my clutch from the nightstand. "Let's go."

He follows me, muttering to himself and shaking his head. "Not sexy? If you were any more sexy, I would come in my goddamn boxers."

Chapter Twenty-One
Two-Million-Dollar Bath

I EXPECTED A hollowed-out building, maybe one of those abandoned spaces where the earth has started reclaiming the land with ivy grown over cracked concrete. There are enough old places in the west side of Tanglewood for that to be possible.

Instead I find a grand old building with cornices and ionic columns and a wide bank of brass doors set in thick wavy glass. Inside there's a marble entranceway and a dome stained-glass ceiling. Only a few panes are broken, petals in the flowers that let in shards of sunlight, illuminating a wealth of dust floating in the air. The whole place is done in an art deco style, original work with brass cage light fixtures and stylized roses in the marble floors.

High wooden countertops line the entrance, where intrepid old Tanglewood citizens would go to ask questions before you could ask Alexa anything on your Amazon Echo. Behind the counter is the focal point, a wall carving that's two stories high—a collage of waves and sky, square-faced men wielding tools and working with the land. It's a story of triumph, that carving. Even an inch deep in dust and with a bird's nest hanging loosely off one of the men's eyebrows, it takes my breath away to look at it.

And through a great curved hallway, shelves and shelves of books.

"Oh my God," I whisper.

"It's something, isn't it?" Sutton says, sounding reluctantly impressed. "Apparently they ran out of funding to pay the librarians, so they just shut the doors one day. Didn't bother to sell off anything inside or use the building for something else."

I wander over to a circular file which has little printed cards where people could write requests. There's one sitting with a half-sized pencil, the words *Crossing the Rubicon* written on it. They really had locked the doors without any notice or closure.

One day there was a functioning library. A center for knowledge and community.

And the next day, nothing.

I whirl on Sutton, remembering what he told me. "'This is more of a teardown and rebuild.'

That's what you said. Are you insane?"

"There's no money in a library," he says, his voice gentle.

It makes me think that maybe he mourns the loss of this place, too. Not enough to go easy on him, though. "No wonder Mrs. Rosemont was pissed at you. This is a travesty."

"That woman has enough money to have restored the library herself if she cared about it that much. It's convenient that she's worried about it now that I own the deed."

"You and Christopher," I remind him. "You own it together."

He laughs. "If Christopher had his way, we would have had a wrecking crew already through here. He doesn't see anything of value between these walls."

There's an uncomfortable symmetry between this old building and me. "And what about you? Do you see any value here?"

He looks up at the broken stained-glass windows, his handsome face in silhouette, revealing a place in his nose where it once must have broken. "It's a beauty, that's for sure. I thought it would be enough of a tribute to build something grand in its place."

"That's not a tribute. That's—that's—"

"A travesty," he says, his voice dry. "You mentioned that. There was an option in the construction plans, an idea I had once to keep the walls and the doors. Even the old style, but most of this would still be cleared to make way for the stores."

"The stores."

"It's going to be a mall. We may not understand the way society ladies work, but we know enough. If there's a Jimmy Choos over where the picture books are, they'll come shop."

"I resign," I say, tossing the empty coffee cup into a trash that's half full with crumpled paper. "And I'm joining the Tanglewood Historical Society."

Sutton doesn't look alarmed by my declaration. Instead he seems pleased, maybe even a little smug. Typical man. "I knew you were the right person for the job."

"Because I'm quitting?"

"Because you aren't going to let us screw this up."

My skin prickles with that sense of a role reversal again, that Christopher is always trying to save me. That Sutton thinks I can save them both, instead. "I'm serious, though. This place is like magic. You can't turn it into a mall."

"We aren't a charity," he reminds me, but his voice isn't a reprimand. Instead it's like we're brainstorming, so I let him lead me deeper into the library. "This has to make money or we just took a two-million-dollar bath."

"No one needs to be that clean," I agree, secretly shocked that they had poured that much money into this place. No wonder Christopher's so bent on starting construction. It would take a serious overhaul to turn this place into a shiny mall with luxury shops.

Sutton pauses to look at a row of plaques that has the names of old families. The brass is tarnished and green now. This is what's become of their legacy.

I walk past him to a great hall that contains books in rows and rows. The dust is dense here, without even the broken stained-glass windows to let in fresh air. It tickles my nose until I sneeze, disturbing the layer of gray on a book beside me. I touch the old cloth spines as I pass, taking away a smudge of dirt with my forefinger, leaving a trail where I've been.

The rows are even enough to follow, but the signage less clear. There aren't any signs above each row to say what's inside. You'd have to ask one of the long-gone librarians to find anything. I keep walking, gradually coming to understand the system for things. Fiction and nonfiction. Memoirs and reference materials. There's a large section on history, which is super meta considering this building has become a slice of the past.

My finger touches books that haven't been read in years, their pages silent in this tomb of a library. Books about the medieval times and the ancient Vikings.

There's a section about Greek and Roman history. There are a few books I skimmed through in Smith College's library. Ancient history doesn't change that much.

One catches my eye. *The Goddess of Egypt*, it says, with a stylized painting that could only be Cleopatra. At least they've drawn her without the asp wrapped around her arm, but she has the classic heavy eyeliner and seductive pose. The Mona Lisa smile.

I flip it open, which sends a cloud of dust into my eyes. They're watering by the time the page comes into focus. The text is small enough to need a magnifying glass, but a sentence in this random place jumps out to me.

It's a testament to female power that she was able to create a shadow of her own beside two men of incredible ambition and renown.

Two men of incredible ambition. I have a little experience with that after last night, though I'm not sure how much of a shadow I create myself. I'm not sure I *want* much of a shadow, considering we know the tragic end that Cleopatra met. History wasn't kind to women who held beauty and power. I'm not sure the present is much kinder.

"What do you think?" comes a low voice behind me.

I gasp in a mouthful of old air and cough. Sutton stands too close to me, his body warm and imposing, somehow making the aisle shrink. "I think you surprised me."

"You fit here, which is strange."

"Strange because I know how to read?" I ask tartly.

"Strange because you're the epitome of the modern woman, but you look so comfortable in this stuffy old library. I think you'd fit in anywhere, wouldn't you?"

"That comes from moving every few months," I say, the words out before I can call them back. I don't usually share that with anyone. Definitely not a man who thinks I'm beautiful and mysterious. "Not that I minded."

He looks grave. "Are you going to settle down

in New York?"

That's where most of the people I know have moved. Or places farther away, like Milan or Bombay. Places to inspire an artist's heart. I never told them that I long for something simpler. Something more like an old library that hasn't been touched in forever.

"Maybe." I snap the book shut and carry it to the front.

He follows, a little bemused. "You're stealing a book."

A gasp of outrage. "I wouldn't steal. I'm checking it out, obviously."

"Should I go behind the counter, then?"

"No one would mistake you for a librarian," I say, glancing wryly at the elegant lines of his suit. How such a large man manages to move gracefully is something physicians can study. Something old Greek artists would have tried to carve out of marble.

I push aside a swinging wooden door to go behind the counter myself. There's a time capsule back here, papers in stacks moved only by the wind from above. Old stools with the leather worn, probably old even when the library closed. What had the librarians done when they closed the doors? Had they mourned this place?

Someone should have.

Sutton follows me behind the counter, his blunt fingers moving along a carving in the back wall. Leaves create a forest wall made out of mahogany. A place for a tired librarian to lean against between moving stacks of books around.

Finally I find the little cards that they would fill out to lend a book. There's a place to write the full name and address of the person. A place to write the book information. An optional ten-cent donation check box. Sutton joins me, placing his hand on my waist—such a small touch. It shouldn't make my heart race.

"Look," I say, showing him. "You can earn back your two million with this."

He bends close, his blond hair more golden in this dim and dusty light. "How many books would we have to lend? It's not as fast of a return as we hoped for."

A sense of lightness invades my chest because he plays along with me. Does that mean he respects me more or less than Christopher, who rejects my ideas right away? I'm not sure either of them see me as an equal, but they both want my body.

Looking down at the cover of Cleopatra, the artist's rendition of an overpriced prostitute done with childish ideas of Egyptian fashion, I wonder if that's all we ever have.

Sutton turns his face toward my neck, breathing in. I turn toward him, my mouth only a few inches away. We could kiss in this place, and it would be almost sacred.

He pulls away, only an inch. Enough. "We can go to the office," he says, his voice rough. "I'll show you the plans and then we can talk about next steps."

So businesslike, those words. Next steps.

I turn so that the counter is against my back and I'm facing Sutton. He could step back, if he really didn't want this. If he didn't want me to grasp his red tie and pull. If he didn't want me to push up on my toes and kiss the corner of his lips.

He groans and opens his mouth over mine. His tongue touches my lower lip, my tongue. He touches me in intimate, warm places, and I can only think about him kissing me between my legs. Especially when his palm lands heavy on my thigh.

"Here?" I ask, but it's not really a question. It's more of a command.

His hands grasp me in a brusque motion, pushing me so that I'm sitting on the counter. My legs open with a naturalness that surprises me, and he moves between them. Even with the way his waist narrows, he spreads me wide. His demanding kiss pushes me back, only an inch, enough to unbalance me. My hands fall back to catch me on the dusty stacks of paper.

"Here," he says as if it's an order.

Both of us know by now that it's acquiescence. He's put me in charge of this thing we're doing, made me the goddess of this ancient library. It makes me feel powerful when I grasp his hair and hold him steady, biting his bottom lip.

His hips jerk, as if against his will, pressing something hard and long against the inside of my leg. It makes me bite him again, harder this time. How does he do this to me? Make me vicious. As if something dangerous inside him calls to me.

And I know that he's strong enough to take anything I give him.

"Do you think," I say, gasping, "there were librarians who did this?"

He moves his mouth to my jaw, making my skin oversensitive with his lips. "God, I hope so. It would have been a travesty to have this counter and not use it."

When he brushes his teeth along my collarbone, I let my head fall back. I look up at the broken windowpanes, at the too-bright sun. "I didn't come last night."

"No?" he asks, nipping at the upper curve of my breast. "You didn't have Christopher finish what I started? You didn't tell him to get on his knees for you?"

"He—" I have to pause and search for words as Sutton pushes his hand, blunt and urgent, beneath my panties. "He wanted to."

That makes him push his clothed cock against me, same as the bite. He likes it when I'm rough with him. We're both animalistic this way, here in this abandoned place.

"Would you touch me now if I'd let him?"

"Hell yes," he says, his voice a grumble, those blue eyes narrowed. "I'd show you that I can make it better. I'm not afraid of competition."

"You like it," I say, panting.

"Yeah," he says, and his fingers find me wet and swollen. His lids lower. He presses an open-mouthed kiss on my belly. Lower, lower. "I like competing. You gonna make me fight for it, honey?"

It's probably wrong to answer yes. There's some moral weakness inside me that only came to the surface when Christopher showed up at L'Etoile last night. "Would you win?" I whisper.

"No chance in hell I'm letting this sweet pussy get away." That drawl becomes stronger when he's turned on. It makes me want to push him further, to see how heavy and thick he can sound. So I spread my legs wider, using my heel on the counter for leverage, pressing myself against his mouth. He grunts his appreciation, spearing me with a blunt finger, and then two. His hand twists and does something inside me, something that makes my mouth fall open.

He pulls back enough to watch his fingers, in and out, in and out.

"Don't stop," I moan, pushing my hips against the air.

He laughs against me, the breath of it a terrible tease. "Did it hurt last night?"

"Evil," is all I can say, especially when he presses a small kiss to my clit.

"My dick hurt like hell," he says, rubbing his thumb against my clit. "Couldn't jerk it because it made me wonder if you were with him. So I had to lie there hard as a fucking rock all night, waiting until it was morning."

"I'm sorry," I say on a moan, but that's a lie. The same way he lies to me. I'm not sorry he hurt for me; it feels like the only compensation in this whole confusing situation. That his cock throbs and aches and wants the way my body does.

"You will be," he says, his voice low and hard-edged. "You'll be sorry when I spank your ass pink with one of these books. Then maybe you'll know better than to tease me."

Surprise squeezes my lungs, because I'm pretty sure he's only pretending. Or maybe he's really going to punish me. My body doesn't seem to care, because I gasp and writhe in his hold, fighting him in this maybe-game we're playing.

Large hands grasp my hips and flip me over like I weigh nothing. Then I'm bent over the counter where a hundred books must have been lent over the years. A thousand books. More?

I'm defiling all of it with my breasts pressed against the dusty wood and my hands clenching in old paper. He picks something up; I feel the whoosh of air where I'm exposed. I tense, but nothing hits me.

"Don't worry," he says in that hard-edge voice that means I should be very worried. "I'm going to warn you before I do it. I want you good and afraid."

"I'm afraid," I whimper.

He shows me the book he has—there are stacks of them haphazard on the counter, books that were returned but never shelved, forever in purgatory. It could have been any one of them, but of course it's *The Goddess of Egypt*. Stylized Cleopatra looks back at me with her mysterious eyes and knowing smile. I'm going to paint her. I'll have to paint her, in some way other than in that seductive pose they always use. Maybe she'll be bent over a table, her body shaking in almost-real fear at the man behind her.

"Ready, honey?" he asks, soft. And I know this is the time when I can speak up. *Don't hit me. I don't want that. I'm not that kind of woman.* But if there's anything last night showed me, it's that I don't know what kind of woman I am. Maybe none of us really do until we have two men fighting for us. Maybe there's a Cleopatra inside each of us.

"Ready," I whisper.

The book makes a whistle sound in the air. It winds something up in my body, something that only springs loose when a flat pain echoes through me. I cry out, more from the surprise than the hurt. A large palm molds itself to my ass, soothing away whatever sting was left.

Another whistle; another cry.

It isn't harder than the jolt of a roller coaster bar against my stomach. It's not the pain that makes this good; it's knowing that he's doing it to me. I'm in this powerless position, because of my lust, because I chose this. Because I chose *him*.

His fingers find me again, slick and ready. It only takes the barest twist, the smallest circle around my clit before I'm coming apart, my legs shaking, every muscle clenched. Pleasure saturates my mind like the yellow-orange rays of sunlight at dawn, breaching the horizon.

The book drops beside me, right in my line of sight. He wants me to see it.

To imagine the imprint of my ass on the old glossy cover.

A small tear behind me, a rustle of cloth. I clench harder on the papers in my fists as if they're rope instead of pointless forms.

He's probably good with rope.

Yes yes yes. He's so good with it he doesn't need anything as primitive as fibers and knots. He has me tied down to this counter with pure force of will—not even his own. Mine. It's my desire that keeps my breasts against the wood, that keeps my ass in the air while he strokes me with callused hands. "One day we'll have to try a bed," he says in that voice that pretends to be unaffected. As if I can't feel his cock throbbing against my thigh.

"Later," I manage to say in a voice just as bland. "To spice things up."

A bark of laughter echoes through the library, sending a bird from its nest of dictionaries and Dickens, a flurry of feathers through the largest broken window. My gaze follows the path, even when there's a wide heat pressing between my legs.

Even when I moan in sudden panic.

He seemed big when I felt him through his slacks, but I wasn't specifically worried about size. Nature has its own geometry, doesn't it? That's what I thought, but now I'm less sure.

He pauses, easing a large hand along my lower back. Settling me back down. "Do you need to come again?" he asks.

The question is so casual, so kind, that I'm struck by my own inexperience. That I could do this in an abandoned library, bent over the counter, with a man who is technically my boss.

"Maybe," I say, but the word is high-pitched and uncertain to my own ears.

A long silence speaks volumes, like the books that surround us, spilling secrets for anyone who pauses to listen. Or anyone bent over a desk, a heavy hand on her lower back, legs shaking.

"Goddamn," he whispers, and he sounds just as unsteady as me.

"Are we still going to have sex? Because if not,

I think I should probably be standing for this conversation." I'm babbling a little. Nervous. *Exposed.*

There's no hurry at all in his movements. He pulls me up and sets my clothes to rights, using hands that don't tremble and a body that doesn't shiver every two seconds. Then he pushes me back so smoothly that I barely realize I'm sitting on the counter again. Mostly I'm sure of it because it no longer feels like I'm about to fall down.

"I don't want…"

He studies me with infinite patience, his blond hair ruffled. Did I pull his hair when he knelt in front of me? Or is that a natural disarray that happens when he has almost-sex? His voice is calm and solid as an oak tree when he asks, "Don't want what?"

"Don't want you to protect me. Don't want you to be the hero and protect my stupid virginity, which is just a social construct, by the way. It doesn't mean anything."

"Harper."

"It's not something I need to be protected from, like it's 1580 and I'm a maiden and my virtue has to be guarded by the men in my family." And I'm so, so tired of being protected by Christopher Bardot. Protected by my father.

Protected by these formidable walls I've built so I don't get my heart smashed to bits.

"*Harper.* I'm not protecting you."

"And it's not like—oh. You're not?"

He laughs, a little rueful. "I'm protecting myself if anything. How do you manage to seem so damned experienced when you're a virgin?"

I make a face. "What does that even mean, experienced? I have life experience. Having a dick inside isn't some kind of transcendent experience. Only a man would think so."

"Only a virgin would think it doesn't matter."

"Look," I say, feeling a little manic. Because maybe I had always imagined it would be Christopher. That seems impossibly naive in the light of a broken stained-glass dome. "I wasn't saving myself for marriage or anything dramatic like that. I just wanted it to be the right place and time. Like an abandoned library, apparently."

"Like eight a.m. on a Friday."

"Apparently," I say, trying to sound worldly. "Maybe I'm a morning-sex kind of girl. I'm not usually awake in the mornings, so I never knew that about myself. See, you do learn things in libraries."

Sutton picks up the book about Cleopatra and hands it to me. "Come on."

"More spankings?"

"No," he says, very severe. Very angry about the virginal spankings. "We're going to the office, where I'm going to show you the damn blueprints."

"Work."

It's a relief that he's focusing on work instead of sex.

And a terrible disappointment.

I think out of any man in the world, Sutton Mayfair is the only one who could make me forget about Christopher Bardot. For even two seconds, forget about the man I've been in love with since I was fifteen years old. It's an allure to someone who's been trapped for so long. A shiny key dangled in front of someone who's been behind bars.

"You have a lot of work to do if you're going to convince the historical society to let us raze this place down."

"You're not razing anything," I say, pushing off the counter and pointing a finger at his chest. "And don't look smug. I'm still turned on, but I'm choosing to ignore that for now and focus on the fact that this library is going to be restored."

"Libraries don't make money," he reminds me, his voice gentle.

CHAPTER TWENTY-TWO
Going Out of Business

I'M ON THE phone with Avery that afternoon, having seen enough architectural diagrams of a modern monstrosity to last me a lifetime. It would be a beautiful mall, one I'd love to shop in if it were located anywhere else in the city.

"What about a bookstore?" I ask, sketching out a Cleopatra reading a book with that Mona Lisa smile on her face. Why can't she look any other way but sultry?

"Oh, that would be cool," Avery says, because she's that kind of friend. Supportive, even when you have dumb ideas. "Aren't bookstores going out of business, though?"

"There's really no way a bookstore can earn back what they put into it, not even if they sell a thousand books a day. Besides, it wouldn't be the same."

"The same as what?"

"This library... I wish you could see it. You'd just die. And probably find some out-of-print book about Helen of Troy to make you have an orgasm right on the spot."

"Mmmm," she says, sounding a little orgasmic at the idea. "What if you create a little museum section in the mall, where it shows some of the old books?"

"So people can put down their slushies and pretzels on the glass case?"

"I don't understand why they even bought a library."

"For the location. And a total lack of respect for old books. They think the mall is going to be some kind of commercial revival for the west side."

She's quiet for long enough that I know she's holding out on me.

"Spill."

"Maybe it really would be good for the city," she says in a rush. "The books aren't doing anyone any good collecting dust. An influx of cash from the rich side of the city might be exactly what the west side needs."

"You've been spending too much time with Gabriel."

"And you still have the books," she says. "You could sell them and use the money to create a new library. A smaller library that has books and a computer lab."

"Way too much time with Gabriel. Now you're practical and boring."

"I forgot to mention you're on speakerphone."

A smile takes over no matter how hard I fight it. "I'm sorry, Gabriel. But I'm sorry in that way where I said something true and I'm only sorry you heard it. You're rubbing off on her."

"That's my favorite thing to do with her," he says, his voice far from the phone.

It makes me laugh, which is what I needed.

Gabriel is a good man, even if he did buy my best friend's virginity as revenge. These things happen. The important thing is that he loves her. She only has to blink at something and he'll pour his fortune into buying it for her. I'm almost certain they won't end in tragedy, but you never really know with love.

That's why I'm better off without it.

Chapter Twenty-Three
Thieves Club

THE DEN IS a place owned by a criminal and bastard, so naturally it's spilling over with patrons when I show up at ten p.m. They wear suits and party dresses, laughter and drinks flowing freely when I step into the foyer. The crowd here is younger and more playful than the gala, but just as rich. Just as powerful in their own corner of the city.

From across the room I see Hugo with his head bent, speaking to Christopher and another man with a shaved head and muscles like whoa. I've never met the third man before. He stands and approaches the bar area, so I sidle up to him.

"Hi," I say, dropping my rose-gold clutch on the mirrored surface.

He looks at me sideways. "Who are you?"

There's a natural command in his voice, the kind that can only come from having been in charge of men for a long stretch of his life. Military? It's in the way he holds himself. "A friend of Beatrix Cartwright. And Avery James."

His eyes are a darker blue than Sutton, more midnight than ocean. "Ah."

"Ah?"

"You're the artist. The one Sutton talks about."

"He talks about me?" My voice comes out high-pitched, because I don't know whether he talks about what happened in the hallway or what happened bent over on the counter. Either way my cheeks burn hot in the company of this stranger. He's wearing a wedding band and he doesn't seem the least interested in me sexually, which only makes it more embarrassing somehow.

"You're going to save the library."

"Oh," I say, relieved. "I'm not sure how, but that's the plan."

"Christopher's going to lose his shit. It was his idea to raze the whole thing down. I think that's the only way he knows how to make something successful."

Is that what he's trying to do with me, tear me down to my roots, to the muscle and bone, to build me into a woman he might actually trust? "That is weirdly insightful, stranger. Almost like you know Christopher really well, but I don't know you."

The corner of his mouth twitches. "Blue Eastman."

"Your name is Blue."

"Yes."

"Like it says that on your birth certificate. Blue like the color."

He laughs a little rusty, like he's not used to doing it. "That's right."

"I'm sorry, I can't really move on. Was Green in the running? If you had been born with green eyes, would you be named Green?"

"Probably." He pauses, accepting a beer that the bartender sends his way. "Do you want anything? Sutton will be annoyed at me that I bought you a drink."

"An old-fashioned," I tell the bartender, a pretty young woman with strawberry-blonde curls and twinkling eyes. "And I'm paying for it."

Blue takes a sip of beer and then considers the amber liquid. "My father had brown eyes. Black hair. My mother had dark skin and even darker hair."

"Babies have blue eyes," I whisper.

"Not in my family. At least that's what my dad said, for all that he didn't know shit about genetics either. So he named me Blue to punish my mother, to always remind her that he knew."

"Wow. Did she actually...?"

"Until the day she died, she maintained that she had never cheated. Which either makes her a dedicated liar or very bad chooser of husbands."

Love is a terrible monster. It seduces you like a siren, pulling you closer even though you know you're going to be smashed to bits against the rocks.

"I'm sorry." What a terrible way to grow up, knowing that every time your parents looked at you, they were thinking about an indiscretion that may never have happened. Finding the proof in your appearance. "No wonder you left and joined the army."

"That obvious?"

"Pretty much. But what I don't know is how you know Christopher. He's not exactly the hoorah, my-biceps-are-bigger-than-yours type. I say that with complete respect, because your biceps are definitely bigger than mine. And also everyone else's."

"We're... friends," he says, the word almost foreign on his lips.

"I didn't know he had friends." Except for Sutton, though I wouldn't have used the word *friends*. They're business partners, sure. Enemies maybe.

Blue nods toward the group of armchairs in the corner where Hugo and Sutton are still talking. "The four of us. I probably shouldn't tell you this, but we sort of ironically, but not ironically, call ourselves the Thieves Club."

"Is it because you steal jewelry at galas? I'm not judging. Anyone would consider it. There's a ridiculous amount of diamonds in a single room."

"It's something Hugo said a long time ago. That every dollar earned was a dollar we took from someone else. Whether we returned a service for that money is beside the point. The amount of money in the world is finite."

There's a rush of air, and then Christopher is on the other side of me, having appeared like some kind of magician. The breath whooshes out of me for a solid five seconds, and when I breathe back in a gulp, the air comes flavored with him— crisp and dark and always so damned comforting when I shouldn't be comforted by him.

"Until the government prints more," he says, the educated economist inside him sounding like Daddy, which unnerves me and comforts me even more. Goddamn it.

Blue tips his glass of beer in greeting. "Though if we took those freshly minted dollars, we really would be the Thieves Club."

"We'll call that plan B," I say, accepting my old-fashioned from the bartender with a murmured thanks. "The gala seems like an easier mark, really."

Christopher is faster than me, sliding a twenty across the mirrored counter before I can pull money out of my clutch. It makes me scowl at him, because it's an extension of the way he tries to control me—handing out and withholding money according to his own code.

"I'm not grateful," I tell him, taking a gulp of the drink.

"I don't expect you to be," he murmurs. "But you don't need to think about stealing. You're one of the richest women in the country."

Blue seems to have evaporated, probably returning to the group of armchairs in the corner. I can't seem to take my gaze away from Christopher's dark eyes to check. There's something different about him tonight, but I can't figure out what.

He looks a little less forbidding.

"A lot of good that does me," I say.

"If you help us push this project through you'll get the money you want."

I look down at my drink. Now I understand why men do this, the broody, staring-at-alcohol thing. It's a moral dilemma, because if I push the project through, I'll help Mom. But I'll also destroy something beautiful in the library.

"Sutton told me," Christopher says, reading my mood correctly. "You're your father's daughter. You know there's no way to make money back on a library."

"Maybe it can be like the Den. You could serve alcohol at the counter while you check out books. And people could discuss philosophy and sex like a modern-day French salon."

"It works for the Den because Damon Scott runs it. It's basically headquarters for his criminal enterprises. Laundering money and selling weapons isn't in our business plan."

"He doesn't sell weapons," the bartender says.

Christopher gives her a small smile. "You would know."

She smiles back with a nod that makes her look like royalty. "I like the idea of selling alcohol at a library. I'd buy a glass of wine to sit with a book, but I'm not sure it will make the kind of money you're looking for."

"This is Penny," Christopher says, giving enough weight to the name that I should know who she is. "She's with Damon Scott. Though I haven't seen her behind the bar before tonight."

"I'm trying my hand at mixing drinks."

"You're good at it," I say with a rueful glance at my empty glass.

She laughs, a tinkling sound. "Thank you. Anyway, it's a good place to eavesdrop on people. That's probably why Damon started a bar in the first place. He sells information."

"I don't suppose you're looking to get into the information business?" I ask Christopher hopefully, even though I wouldn't like him half as much if he did. He operates on his own code of honor, which is warped and broken but comes from a good place.

"Fashion and trendy electronics at a high markup would be preferable."

"I could buy it from you," I say, which suddenly seems like the best idea. "It would be my personal library, so it follows the rules of the trust fund. And I'd give you whatever you paid for it. More, even. So it would still make money for you."

"That's assuming I would sell it to you," he says, almost gently now. That's what's different about him. There's no derision in his expression. Less coldness in his voice. He's almost, *almost* human. And he sounds apologetic, as if he wished he didn't have to disappoint me.

"I'm not going to beg." Mostly because I know it won't do any good with him. I've already tried that, when I was far more desperate than I am now.

"I'm not selling it, for many reasons. The location of the library was calculated based on many different factors. We won't find another place ripe for gentrification like this one."

"Why do you care so much about gentrification?"

"Because it's going to make me a rich man."

"If you had two million dollars to put into it, you're already a rich man."

"One million," he says. "Sutton put in the other half. And a million dollars doesn't make you a rich man in this economy. There's more in the trust to maintain the damn yacht."

"Good Lord. How much does it cost to wax the deck?"

Christopher gives me a half smile that looks so much like him as a college boy that my heart skips a beat. "That depends on how shiny you want it."

"The library is a monument to knowledge and community and the irrepressible spirit of mankind. You can't just tear it down and build a mall."

"Malls are irrepressible. And profitable."

There's no way I can save the library. Failure makes my chest feel tight, which isn't a totally new feeling. Especially when I'm in Christopher's presence. Why do I always feel crushed when he walks away? And why do I keep seeking him out, even though I know how it will end?

I can't save the library, but the worst part is I'm not sure I can save the mall project either. We would have to convince the historical society to let us build it.

Another cocktail appears in front of me, sent by the too-knowing Penny with sympathetic brown eyes. I take a large swallow of my cocktail, enough that even this top-shelf liquor makes my throat burn.

"You can use the office," Christopher says. "Invite them over and show them the plans. I don't mind letting them see, but I'm not going to change a damn thing."

"There's the spirit of compromise and community that will endear you to them."

Penny shines a perfectly clean glass with a rag, managing to look conspicuous as she does it. "I don't mean to interrupt, but I've met some of the women in the historical society."

"Are you friends with them?" I ask hopefully.

"I wouldn't go that far, but I like to think I

know how they operate. And if you bring them into a boardroom and show them documents that are already drafted, they're going to say no."

"That's what I'm thinking, too. And the worst part is I don't totally disagree with them. It's a gorgeous building. It should be lovingly restored, not torn down for the land."

Christopher gives me a dire look. "And Sutton asks why I don't think it's a good idea, you being our liaison with them. Maybe because you're not on our side."

"I'm not on anyone's side," I tell him, annoyed. "I'm on my own side. There's only me on this side. You and Sutton, you're not invited."

A smile plays on Penny's lips. "Did you hear about the show that's come to the Grand? It's sold out on Broadway, with limited tour dates, so it's a coup that we got a stop. One night only. Tomorrow night."

The implications run through me like warm water. Mrs. Rosemont may have asked to hear details about the project, but it won't help to show them to her. Those councilmen that are holding the permits in perpetual review? They'll nix them for good. "So everyone will be there. Can we get tickets?"

"It's been sold out for weeks. Damon and I

have been looking forward to it since we heard. And I happen to have a couple of extra seats in my box." She glances sideways where Sutton sits, watching us now with an unreadable expression. "Only two, but we know the owners of the theater. They'll let us add another chair to the box."

"Thank you *so much*," I say, clapping. "This will be perfect."

Christopher sounds droll. "I don't suppose you'd accept money in exchange for the seats."

She laughs. "Of course not. You'll owe us a big favor, because if there's one thing Damon Scott loves collecting more than information, it's favors."

Chapter Twenty-Four
Gold Standard

"**H**E HAS *FRIENDS*," I tell Avery, on my bed and staring up at the chandelier hanging from the ceiling. I took a cab back to L'Etoile, refusing to let either Sutton or Christopher bring me home.

"He's probably had friends before."

"I don't know." I remember how he looked bent over his textbook, forlorn and serious and determined. "He may have given his textbooks names and had whole conversations with them."

"You just never lived in the same city as him," she says.

"Did you know about this Thieves Club? That's what they call themselves, Sutton and Christopher and Hugo. And this man whose name is Blue, like the color."

"Because they steal jewels from the bank?"

"That's what I asked!" This is why talking to Avery grounds me. She understands me like no one else. Besides she asked for the scoop, which is only fair since she gave me the tip about going to the Den. "Apparently it's because every dollar they earn is one taken from someone else and money is finite or something."

"Hmm," she says. "So he has friends and you met them. Does that mean he's human now, instead of a big symbolic version of your dad you can hate?"

"Don't psychoanalyze me," I say in a singsong voice. "Two can play at that game and you *sold* your virginity in a public auction, so you're always going to be weirder."

That earns me a laugh. "So you're going to the theater tomorrow."

"And I still have no idea what I'm going to say to Mrs. Rosemont. *Hey, the library is a gorgeous piece of history. Can we have your blessing to burn it down?*"

"Burning it seems inefficient. Won't there just be a wrecking ball or bulldozer or something?"

"In my head it's going to be burned like the libraries at Alexandria. And then Christopher will fire me. And Sutton will spank me. And my mom probably won't even do the experimental treatment even if I can get the hospital to let her in after this."

"There will be other libraries," she says gently.

I swallow down the acid that threatens to come up, ruining the pretty lace bedspread. "You're right. The treatment is the most important thing."

This reminder could not be more important. The treatment is more important than making Christopher Bardot jealous. More important than seeing if Sutton Mayfair can be the man who might actually replace him in my heart. More important than the library and painting and anything else in the world. That's the kind of focus that gets things done.

It's the kind of focus that's kept me alive in the cold years since the will reading. Having some goal set for me, however impossible it seemed. Making a living for Mom while going to college. Finding some peace despite the mockery the media made of us.

The butterfly garden was a natural extension of everything that came before. Useful and elaborate and slightly over the top.

There will be other libraries. "Is this how men feel when they sell their morals?"

"It's how I felt," she says, and I know she's thinking of her time at the Den.

"I'm sorry. I wish you'd have come to me then." She's able to laugh about it now, mostly because that's how she found Gabriel Miller. It was terrible at the time.

"And I wish you would fly to the Emerald right now instead of going there tomorrow. We can eat popcorn and watch *Mean Girls* and talk about how boys suck. And then you can tell me about Sutton *spanking* you, which I did not overlook by the way."

"There was possibly a thing with a dusty old book."

"Oh my God."

"And a library counter."

"So you guys are officially… you know. Doing it."

"We've done some things," I say, as breezy as if I've done every single thing on the sexual menu. Repeatedly. "Not all of them. He's very skilled with his hands. And his mouth."

Avery doesn't precisely know that I'm a virgin.

She thinks I've had sex because she knows I go into bedrooms with frat boys and let them hang socks on the door, so it's a reasonable assumption. But I've perfected the art of listening to their troubles and keeping all my clothes on. I've also perfected the art of a hard kick to the balls in case one of them gets particularly persuasive.

Like I told Sutton, I don't think one particular act matters that much. I never thought I was saving it for marriage, but in my head, when I touch myself at night, it was always a dark head of hair and black eyes that looked down on me. Always the same.

No matter how much I hated him, Christopher was always the gold standard.

"He's fun to play with while I'm in town," I say, still casual, because I'd like to have casual virginity-removing sex with Sutton. Then I can stop the stupidity of imagining Christopher being my first. "Not anything serious."

"Oh my God, Harper." She sounds scandalized. "Two men?"

"No," I correct sharply. "There's only one man. Even that is temporary."

Temporary, the word my mother used to describe my father's wives. And her husbands.

Nothing lasts forever.

"Two men," Avery says, insistent. "There's always been something between you and Christopher. Mostly you two have never stayed in the same city long enough to do anything about it. And now he's seeing you with his business partner..."

Seeing me with my dress up around my waist, my sex exposed in the hallway while his business partner licks my pussy. "Nothing is going to happen."

"But call me when it does."

"I'm literally never going to call you again, because nothing is going to happen."

"Okay," she says, not believing me for a second. "Talk to you tomorrow."

I hang up with an exasperated smile, tossing the phone onto the nightstand. I'm feeling a little punchy without any of my supplies with me, but I don't want to make a trip to the art store.

For one thing I don't think the concierge would take kindly to me splashing oil-based paint all over their antique furniture and old wallpaper. I also don't want to imply, even to myself, that I'll be staying in Tanglewood for longer than a few days. I'll sort out the issue with the Tanglewood Historical Society and be back in LA with my mother and her new treatment and my brushes.

The only thing of interest in the hotel room is the book on Cleopatra, which is more interesting than the cover could possibly imply. There's intrigue in here about her life, going beyond her experiences with Julius and Antony. Chapters and chapters from before she was ever a glint in their eyes. The making of a powerful woman, through the only means available to her.

Those men, who wanted her for her body. And her mind?

Did they think they were in love with her?

She was more than a pretty face to them, this much we know. They used her, and she used them back. And in the end she outlasted them both, so maybe that's the moral of the story.

It ended in tragedy for all three of them, though.

Maybe that's the true moral of the story.

CHAPTER TWENTY-FIVE
My Father's Daughter

THE GRAND FITS its name with a gorgeous fountain in the front and ornate carving along the front that's been lovingly repaired with plaster. Old trees surround the property like an embrace. A thick red carpet covers the cobblestone close to the entrance.

"See?" I tell Sutton, who looks ridiculously handsome in a suit. "This is how you treat a place with history. You don't blow it up into a million pieces."

"We aren't going to blow up the library," he says, that rough voice underlaid with amusement. "And besides, I don't think this is the example we should follow. The Grand used to be a strip club."

Through an arched doorway I can see gilded wood box seats and a wide stage. "And you know this by rumor only, I'm sure. It's not that you would have gone to a strip club yourself."

He laughs in a fully masculine way that does not confirm or deny anything. "I work with the construction company that did some of the restoration."

It's almost impossible to believe that this place was anything but a theater. It's cleaner and more elegant than some of the theaters I've been to on Broadway, which maybe isn't saying much. "Some businesspeople clearly value culture."

"Ivan Tabakov values beautiful women," Sutton says. "Especially the beautiful woman he married, who was herself a stripper until they converted it to a theater. Or back to a theater, I should say, since that's how it started."

"That's what the mall would be," I say, quiet so only he can hear.

"A strip club?"

"I'm not judging the women who worked here, but there's a reason they converted it back. Because desperation and money and sex are not the answer."

"Hey," he says, laughing silently. "Leave sex out of this."

I look at the ceiling, at the dark wood beams and the faded pink textured wallpaper. They're original to this place; I can feel it in my bones. "I'm not bashing malls or strip clubs," I say, still looking up. "I'm not even bashing money, but it's a problem when you have to destroy something beautiful to have them."

When I glance back at Sutton, his expression is grave. "What other beautiful things have you seen destroyed?" he asks softly.

I don't answer him, but I think he already knows. My mother's dignity. My own innocence. The better question is, what beautiful things does money *not* destroy? It touches everything with its dirty hands, marking us, leaving us weaker than before.

"There they are," he murmurs, nodding toward a box to the right of the stage.

It's the one with the best view, of course. The best view of both the stage and the rest of the theater. Seats fit for royalty. Penny transformed from a bartender in a crisp white button-down to a gorgeous asymmetrical lilac gown of different textures. The man beside her must be Damon Scott, the angles of his face severe as he surveys the crowd.

And beside them is Christopher, murmuring softly to Damon. Probably making a backroom deal. That's why men come to these things, isn't it? It's an excuse to do business.

Of course I can't blame the gender, since that's why I'm here.

"Wait," I say, when Sutton moves to escort

me toward the stairs. Half the seats are full with people settled in, chatting and flipping through the program. The other half of the seats are still empty, waiting for the people who are milling around or still out with their glasses of champagne.

It takes a few minutes, but finally I spot Mrs. Rosemont when she turns to glance up at the balcony. She's sitting with an older man who I'm guessing is her husband. They have seats right up front. Not quite as glamorous as the box seats, but definitely expensive.

Sutton gives me a curious look but lets me lead us down the row toward them. Maybe he thinks I'm going to sit down and have a chat with her about the library in the ten minutes before the curtain rises, but I'm about two percent more subtle than that. Instead I stand in the aisle, half turned away, flipping through the program they gave us at the door.

Finally the couple beside the Rosemonts stands and makes their way to the exit, probably taking a potty break so they don't have to stand in a monumentally long line during intermission.

"Excuse me," I say when they reach us, sounding nervous and flushed, which isn't that difficult since I'm trembling. "I know this is forward of me, but my brother's in the show tonight."

I spin a story of my brother, the understudy, who's been part of the cast since they started touring. But this will be his first show. They gave us seats, of course, but they're all the way up in the boxes. I want him to be able to see me when he looks out at the audience. There are little touches I pulled from the program—a name of an understudy and the part he'll play.

The woman looks only a few years older than me, and not particularly pleased at the idea of switching seats. She seems the suspicious sort, which is reasonable considering I'm conning them. It's when the husband sees exactly which box they'd be in that things change.

"Is that Damon Scott?" he says, trying to hide his excitement.

"Oh, he's very kind. He's the one who gave us the seats. But my brother will be disappointed if he can't see me in the audience. I promised to wave at him."

So that's how we end up sitting next to the Rosemonts.

I can feel Sutton shaking with laughter beside me, but he manages to hold any words inside. "You hired me to do a job," I tell him under my breath. "I'm doing a job."

"I have no complaints," he murmurs, his hand finding mine.

I let him hold my hand because that's the part we're playing for Tanglewood society right now. Not because it feels warm and comforting for him to rest my palm against his. Not because it's strangely sensual for him to rub his thumb along the outer edge of my hand.

The lights dim without me exchanging a single word with Mrs. Rosemont. We watch the show, which I fully intend to enjoy since I haven't seen it yet. The rave reviews are fully deserved, and I'm laughing and gasping along with the rest of the audience.

She notices me first during intermission, but I'm careful not to look her way. I feel her think about saying something to me two different times. *Didn't we meet at the gala?* she would ask.

But she's silent and so I don't say anything either. Patience.

It's in the final act that things really progress, and by that I mean—I cried. Twice. The show is a gorgeous tragedy, and there are tears streaming down my face. The program is clenched in my hands, almost torn apart by the strength of my emotion. Sutton looks stoic beside me, but I know he's moved by the way he holds my hand.

Mrs. Rosemont is crying, too. When the curtain falls and the actors take their bows, she and I are among the first to rise to our feet, clapping our hands as hard as we can, trying to convey everything we felt and lost and learned in such a basic, universal sound.

It's only when the lights go up again, and everyone streams out the doors, that she turns to me. "You're the one who wants to tear down the library," she says, her eyes tinged red.

"I don't." Lying works well for getting someone to switch seats with you. For something like this, honesty is the only way. "I'd love to restore the library, to see it in its glory."

"Then how can you…" She glances at Sutton but must think better of what she's going to say about him. He sits with his ankle over his knee, looking supremely relaxed and confident in a theater. He would look this way in a stable or a boardroom. That's because it comes from inside him, that certainty that he's right where he needs to be.

"I love the library, but it's not doing anyone any good with all the books molding and the wood rotting. And no one, not Bardot and Mayfair, not the city of Tanglewood, is going to pay the small fortune it would cost to repair it."

She sniffs. "That doesn't mean I'm going to condone a mall."

"What I'm proposing is something that will benefit the city of Tanglewood, the *history* of Tanglewood, more than an abandoned building ever could."

The wrinkles around her eyes deepen. "What is your plan?"

"We go through the books. Find the ones that are worth keeping and the ones that aren't. Donate the ones of value to the Tanglewood library system for distribution or display."

"That's not enough."

This feels like more than an interest in historical restoration. It feels personal. "Tell me why," I say. "Tell me why the library is so important to you."

She studies the velvet curtain, clearly deciding how much to tell me. Secrets are a form of currency. "I went to that library as a child." A pause. "It was more than a place for books, you understand. It was the place you could learn things, no matter what family you came from. No matter how much money you had."

"There are other libraries." It's strange feeling to argue against myself.

"Not like that one."

"Not like that one," I have to concede. "But the books can be restored and find new homes in libraries around the city. Bardot and Mayfair would be honored to fund restoration of some of the best pieces, for better preservation and display."

She mulls that over, her shrewd eyes on the curtained stage, probably imagining how it would look. Not only the value, but the fact that the Tanglewood Historical Society had managed to secure it for the city. It would be a win. "I'll have to talk about it with some of the others. I'm not making any promises."

"There was a library I went to," I tell her, cashing in my own secrets. The times between husbands. "We mostly wouldn't talk to the librarians unless the computers broke. The machines told us where to find books. Then one day I went in and there was a brand new book about Leonora Carrington, the glue still tacky where they'd put the library label on. I could barely find a few lines and one photo of her work in the other books."

"An artist?" Sutton asks, his voice soft.

"A painter. A surrealist." None of those words accurately convey what she meant to me. "She painted mythological creatures, but they're...

they're these radical statement about existence, about transformation, about sexuality. She's the reason I believed I could be a painter."

Sutton makes a small sound and squeezes my hand.

"But there was nothing—no store where you could walk in and buy a book about her or a print of one of her paintings. It was like, in the world of money and power, she never existed."

I don't share that she was expelled from multiple schools for wild behavior. That she was a revolutionary and a vocal feminist. Her family never understood her desire to be an artist.

Sometimes it's an act of rebellion to simply exist.

"My father was a carpenter," Mrs. Rosemont says, her throat working. "Kitchen cabinets and basic furniture, that kind of thing. He never made anything artistic at home. I wouldn't have known it was even inside him, if it weren't for the library."

A thump in my heart. "He made the wall?"

"They paid him twenty dollars for the whole project."

"Oh my God. I can't believe your father made that. It's incredible."

She shakes her head. "It broke my heart when

they shut down the library. But it's always been there. Waiting, I think. Waiting for someone who cares enough."

I look at Sutton, who's watching me with unreadable blue eyes. He's waiting for someone who cares enough, maybe. Waiting for me. We might not be able to save the whole library, but we can save the wall. And it will be better—much better to preserve it properly than let it sit in that dusty, abandoned space, exposed to the elements through the broken glass dome.

"As it happens the extraction and transportation of walls has been a subject of particular interest to me. And Sutton's a carpenter, too. I'm sure we can find a way to pull them off the building and move them… " Where? "Maybe a museum."

"City hall," Mrs. Rosemont says, and I know we've won.

Sutton gives me a small nod of agreement. We still have to convince Christopher, who I think will be less amenable, but I have to believe I can do it. There's a cost to what I'm proposing, but nothing in life is free. Being a stated supporter of the society will mean the project has their backing. It might even help smooth along some of the red tape.

This is the way business is done.

Like Christopher said, I am my father's daughter.

Mrs. Rosemont nods once. "I still have to discuss it with the other members, but this might be the best option. We'll be in touch with some specifics."

That's a nice way of saying she's going to make us bleed through the nose for some expensive book restorations, but I can't really blame her. My job is far from done. There will be more negotiations, but this is a solid start.

Sutton stands. "Shall we?"

He helps me up, but my foot has fallen asleep from sitting too long. I stumble a little against the chairs in front of me. It's Sutton who helps pull me upright, Sutton who keeps me that way when my leg threatens to give out again. Sutton who leans down so that his face is only an inch away from mine, an intimate pose considering we're sitting in one of the front rows of the theater.

Most of the seats are empty now anyway, but there's one man at the back. In the shadows. Of course he would be there. I recognize his silhouette immediately. Christopher must have come down from the box seat and waited for us.

I lean on Sutton as we make our way to the

back.

Vaguely I'm aware of Mrs. Rosemont and her husband trailing after us up the long carpeted aisle. We're almost completely alone in such a large space. The stage is silent after being so full of life for the past three hours. Through the archway I can hear the buzz of voices, people excited and a little tipsy, but they seem far away.

Even a few feet away from Christopher, he's too dark to read. I can feel the tension radiating off him. Is he worried I said something wrong? He steps forward, only half a foot, and I can see his black eyes flash with fury.

"Christopher?" I say, suddenly uncertain. It had felt so natural to make a deal with Mrs. Rosemont with Sutton beside me. This is what I would have done for my father, if he had lived long enough to use me for this. It's what I was born to do.

"I'll take you home," he says, his voice so low it's almost guttural. The sound of a cello in the orchestra pit, foreboding and grave. It means the main actor is in trouble.

Sutton's hand tightens on me, and I realize what this is. Another one of their damn pissing matches. I'm not even sure it matters who I am— it could be anything they're pulling between them. "I've got her," he says, nice and quiet. Lethal in a different way.

"This wasn't a date," I whisper. "I'm not going home with either of you."

Christopher looks away, his jaw ticking. "Of course. We can go to the office instead. You can give me the rundown of what you promised Mrs. Rosemont."

I take a step back, stung. "We can do that tomorrow morning. And hopefully by then you'll have cooled down enough not to speak to me like I'm a child."

A dark gaze slides down my body. The emerald wrap dress suddenly feels like nothing. "You're not a child, Harper. You know exactly what you're doing."

The man was saying a thousand things with the innuendo in his voice, none of it good. I'm struck speechless a moment, wondering how I got to this place. Wondering how I can say anything at all when my throat itches and burns like I might start crying—for a third time tonight.

It's Sutton who steps forward. "I don't know what the hell's wrong with you right now, but you're going to walk away before I remind you how to speak to a woman."

There's nothing leashed about the violence in

his voice. He's about one second from punching his business partner in a public place, even if we're mostly alone.

Mostly, except where's Mrs. Rosemont? Is she seeing this?

"Let's go," I manage in a harsh mutter, though I'm not sure whether I'm talking to Sutton or Christopher. Maybe I'm only talking to myself. "Let's just get out of here."

"Hell," Christopher says softly. "I'm sorry, Harper."

"It doesn't matter," I lie, because it does. There's a hole in my heart that proves it does. "We can talk about the library tomorrow."

He gives a hard shake of his head. "Not that. I'm sorry about the trust fund. I should have let you do whatever the fuck you wanted with it. I shouldn't have let a dead man control you."

There's too much to take in, the fact that Christopher is maybe softening toward me after years of being a hard-ass. The fact that he called Daddy a dead man. Because it wasn't Daddy controlling me, not really. It was Christopher, all along.

I take a step back, away from him. Away from Sutton.

I'm halfway ready to run down the velvet-covered aisle, to climb onstage and through the curtains. Into a fictional world that's just as tragic as my own.

Christopher steps forward, fully in the light, and I realize that he's more than soft. He's drunk. That's why he's saying this. That's why he's being a man I don't even know.

A man I wished existed for so long, it's painful to see this parody of him now.

"Damn you," I whisper.

It happens so fast. Christopher reaching for me, his eyes almost translucent. Showing me things I've always wanted to see, a longing so deep it reaches through my ribs and squeezes.

And then Sutton blocking him, a swift arm to keep me safe.

I can't even tell who swings first, not really. A scream escapes me when I see Christopher's head knocked back in a punch. Then he swings at Sutton. Soon they're on the carpeted floor, rolling around, their black-and-white suits flying, their eyes fierce as animals.

It could have lasted an eternity, that fight.

Or maybe only a few seconds.

Other men come and tear them away. Dimly I recognize Blue as one of them, looking fierce. And another man, his face so hard-set he looks like stone.

There are tear tracks down my cheeks.

I notice them only when they feel cold in the theater air, the rest of my skin flushed. Finally the men calm enough that they are let loose, both of them panting and bloodied. "This is what we've come to," I say, soundless so no one hears me.

This is what we've come to, because of money and sex. Maybe it was inevitable that I would make the same mistake as Mom, but twice as bad.

Two men to trample my dignity instead of one.

Through the shimmer of tears I see Mrs. Rosemont's face pinched as she looks at Christopher and Sutton. I know what she sees. Two men who are out of control.

And the woman who made them this way.

Our eyes meet, and she lifts her chin. *The deal is off,* those shrewd eyes tell me from across the room. No amount of book restorations or carving installations will save us now. No amount of money will repair the trust we've broken.

I should have let her go, but I imprinted early on humiliation.

"Wait," I tell her, wiping my cheeks, useless because they must be streaked with black. "I'm sorry. Don't judge them by this, please. It was a bad night. A strange night."

"I'm not judging them," she says, her voice as stiff as starch. "I'm judging you."

"Yes," I say, pleading now. "It's my fault, not theirs."

I don't actually know whose fault it is or if blame is a thing we can own. It doesn't matter, because my heart is with Christopher and his ambition. My heart is with Sutton and the wild horse he tamed. My heart is in that library, but even that I was willing to give up for these two men. Of course it's love. Only love could hurt this much.

"I was young once," she says. "So I'll tell you this. Sometimes you need to walk away. Maybe you don't see it right now, but those boys are dangerous. They will tear apart anything in their path to get what they want. Even you."

CHAPTER TWENTY-SIX

Mr. Valedictorian

BLUE OFFERS TO take me back to the hotel, but there's a pretty young woman with tired eyes and a large, pregnant belly who waits to the side, so I tell him no. Penny also offers to escort me back, but Damon Scott kind of terrifies me, which is saying something considering the two men who fought each other in front of me.

Sutton's lip has been split, but when I reach up to hover over it, he doesn't flinch. Still in shock, maybe, like he's fallen into the bay and been dragged out. Or maybe he's fought too many times in his life to be shocked anymore. "I'll take you home," he says.

I swallow hard. "I'm not... I'm not the kind of girl that men fight over."

He shakes his head, a quick dismissal. "That says more about us than it does about you. And nothing good, that's for damn sure."

"Does that mean you're going to apologize to him?" Christopher stands only six feet away from us, leaning against the curved stone edge of the fountain, staring out at the city's skyline. It shouldn't be possible to see his expression in this darkness, but I can tell from the set of his shoulders that he's melancholy. It makes me long for the hard-edged, cold Christopher.

The one who breaks my heart but doesn't look melancholy.

"No," Sutton says. "But I'm not going to punch him again. Not tonight."

"I suppose that's the best I can do, but I can't leave him like this. I'm pretty sure he drove here."

Hard blue eyes study the solitary figure. "We can call him a cab."

When did it become Christopher against me and Sutton? Maybe from before I even met Sutton. I would have aligned myself with anyone against Christopher. Does that mean what I have with Sutton, this connection, the invisible string that draws me toward him, isn't real?

"I can't leave him here," I say finally, resigned that I won't figure out the secrets of the heart tonight. "The way he is now. There's too much history."

A sleek black limo glides into the courtyard. Sutton's limo.

I put my hand on his arm, feeling the restraint

in his muscles, the heat of his body. "It's okay. I'll take an Uber with him. You don't have to do anything."

He looks increasingly remote, the more I try to reassure him. "Bring him."

Into the limo? Sutton may have promised not to punch Christopher again, but I'm not sure putting them in a closed metal box going eighty miles per hour is the answer. "We couldn't."

An impatient wave of his hand. "It's the fastest way. The safest, too."

I can't argue with those points, and I don't really relish waiting for an Uber in the dark, making small talk with a random stranger—or Christopher, who seems like a stranger.

He looks up at the stars as I approach him, unmoving even though he must hear my heels on the cobblestone, the red carpet rolled up and put away until there's another show.

"Come on," I say softly. "Let's get you home."

"I'm not drunk," he says, gesturing to the sky as if that proves a point.

"Well, you're not sober."

"Go on ahead. I'm not good company tonight." A humorless laugh bounces off the stone and water of the fountain. And abruptly falls silent.

I put my hand on his arm, feeling his muscles—so different from Sutton. Sleek where he's bulky. Tense where Sutton is deceptively casual, reserving his strength for when he needs it. "I don't have a red and white life preserver, but there's a limo that will work just as well."

He glances over. "Don't think Sutton would appreciate that."

"It was his idea."

Christopher remains still, considering. I wonder what scales are in his head right now, weighing the cost of being near me and Sutton. Weighing the return on investment of a ride home.

I take a step away, hoping he'll follow. "Remember what you said to me? Can you climb? I need you to climb right now, Christopher. One rung at a time."

His eyes are as deep and fathomless as the bay was that night. There might have been sharks in that depth. Or it might have been my imagination, running wild. In the end he stands up and runs a hand through his hair. "We didn't hurt you," he says like a statement, even though it's a question.

"I'm fine." That's a lie, but there are no bruises on my skin. Nothing he can see.

On the inside I'm hurt in ways I didn't know were possible.

It's natural for me to lie, I almost believe the words myself. From the time I was little I had to tell Daddy I was fine or risk losing my mom. I had to lie to Mom or watch her fall apart. Lying is how I keep the world together. It's how I survive.

Sutton has the door open for us when we walk up. He stands a few feet to the side as we get in, both Christopher and me in the very back. Sutton slides in toward the driver, facing us. A rap on the roof, and then we're driving through downtown Tanglewood. We start the drive in almost-silence, only the muffled sound of the tires on the road to soothe us.

"How much of that champagne did you drink?" I finally ask.

"Damon Scott has his own bartender," Christopher says. "Who kept refilling my drink. And I kept drinking it, which is damn stupid of me. I've done a lot of stupid things."

"Okay, Mr. Valedictorian. Clearly you're a sad drunk. That's something I didn't know about you. And now that I know it, you aren't allowed to have liquor."

"He's never held it well," Sutton murmurs from the other seat.

"Really?" I ask, curious about this lightweight side of Christopher.

Sutton looks at me, his blue eyes dark across the limo. "It's not something he does often. In fact this is only the second time I've seen him get drunk. The first time—that was the night we met."

"Hell," Christopher says. Only that.

"We were at the Den," Sutton says. "He told me about this woman he knew."

My throat goes tight, because I know which woman he's talking about. Which means that Christopher was as messed up about me as I was about him. Part of me had suspected that, but it was easier to think of him as an unfeeling robot-monster instead of a flesh-and-blood man.

There's no jealousy in Sutton's blue eyes—well, maybe a little. But mostly understanding. He wasn't clueless when he stepped between us. Definitely not clueless when he bent me over the library counter and spanked my ass with a book.

"What do we do now?" I ask, sounding lost to my own ears.

It's Christopher who answers, his voice bleak. "What we've always done. We work. We fix what's broken. We fight for every goddamn penny."

"Your choice," Sutton says, softer. "It's always been your choice what you do here. Whether you go or stay. And which one of us you bring home."

I swallow hard, because I already know what I'm going to do. For tonight, at least. Christopher has been a rock of ambition the entire time I've known him. Whatever the reason, tonight broke him. I'm not going to leave him alone to face this himself.

The limo pulls up to a high-rise condo. I know from the sleek glass and the stiff bellhop who lives here, even before Christopher pushes out of the seat. Where does Sutton live? Maybe not somewhere as rustic as a ranch, but I know he must be able to open a window. Must be able to feel the sun and the wind on his face.

Christopher walks away from the limo without a backward glance. He doesn't expect me to follow. Maybe he never wants to see me again.

He didn't shiver alone in my cabin after pulling me out of the bay.

"I'm sorry," I say, my voice low in the back of the limo.

Sutton's blue eyes flash. "You're going with him."

Part of me wants to reassure him—*I'm not going to sleep with Christopher. I'm only going to make sure he drinks a glass of water and falls asleep in a bed.* But I don't owe that promise to Sutton. And I can't be one hundred percent sure I'll keep it.

"I'll call you tomorrow," I say instead, four words that mean four thousand things. They mean there's something between us, Sutton and me. Something deep and sensual and ancient. They mean I'm loyal to him, as much as I can be, but the debt I owe Christopher is even older than that.

Sutton's grip tightens on the leather enough that it creaks under his hold. He's a mythical beast, barely held by social constraints. "Let me take you to L'Etoile. Or back to my place. Hell, I'll take you anywhere you want to go."

Except being with Christopher is where I need to go tonight.

"I'll call you tomorrow," I say again, softer now. This time the words mean something different. *I'm sorry.* That's what they say.

Sutton accepts my apology in cold silence. He steps out of the limo to help me stand, offering his hand when my ankle wobbles on the pavement. Even in anger he won't let me fall.

I'VE CONTEMPLATED WHERE Christopher Bardot lives more times than I care to admit. The depths of hell, I would have said once. Looking at the sterile high-rise condominium with its glass surfaces and its black leather, I think I had it right.

In the fridge I find old take-out containers and a bottle of champagne, unopened, that someone must have given him. It takes some searching to find a drawer with some medicine. I pour him a glass of tap water and hand him two Advils. "Take this."

He swallows it without looking at it close or thinking too hard about it. This Christopher is a stranger, one who does what I ask and apologizes for being a bastard. "Thanks."

And says thank you, apparently.

I study his dark eyes, wondering if he fell over the side of the balcony when I wasn't looking and hit his head. "Are you sure you're okay? Sutton didn't knock something loose in the fight?"

He laughs, a little distant. "Deserved it, if he did."

A curved leather couch takes up most of the living space. Christopher stumbles over to it and lies down, and I realize then that I probably won't have much luck moving him. So I follow him over and sit down by his head, moving a lock of dark hair out of his eyes.

"You scared me," I say, soft and serious.

He looks up at me. "Same."

That shakes a silent laugh out of me. "Okay, but I wasn't the one acting crazy."

"No, you were the one holding his hand. The whole damn play, that's all I could see. There could have been an explosion on that stage, and I wouldn't have noticed."

My cheeks feel hot. "That's a shame, because it was an amazing play. About love and betrayal and redemption. About doing what's right, and all the ways we pay for it."

"That's what I saw, too."

He's talking about Sutton holding my hand. Is that the love or the betrayal? Maybe it's the redemption, being saved from the terrible pattern we were in.

"I didn't come to your condo to have sex with you."

He smiles a little, his eyes closed. "Didn't think so. You restrained yourself plenty of other times when I didn't smell like liquor and hadn't just ruined your nice business deal."

"You couldn't hear that from the back."

"No, but I saw the way Sutton looked. What

did you have to promise them?"

"Some book restorations. Saving the carving behind the library. It doesn't matter now. She looked pretty pissed about the fight."

"We'll push the deal through."

"How?" I ask, almost soundless.

He hears me anyway. "I don't know."

"If you're fighting the rich old ladies of the historical society, who's going to buy the designer purses and overpriced shoes when your mall opens?"

He doesn't answer, and I realize he's fallen asleep. A lightweight, my Christopher. Or maybe he just drank his weight in vodka in that box.

The linen closet looks downright pathetic with only a spare sheet and a mismatched blanket. I take them both because I'm already shivering in the condo. The thermostat looks like it would require an airplane pilot to navigate, so I cover Christopher with both of them.

He snores. Not very loud, but enough that I notice. A rumble in his chest. That's an intimate piece of knowledge I never had before, not even when we shared a bed that first night. I was too out of it after my dip in the bay to wake up. Or maybe I heard him and just didn't remember.

It's possible that I snore, that he heard me do

it that night.

This was his fall into the ocean. Not a literal tumble with a splash in the salt water, but a fall nonetheless. The lowest I've ever seen him. How could I not help him back up?

Part of me wants to search his cabinets and drawers to ferret out his secrets. The other part of me realizes that there wouldn't be any lying around. He's a man who holds it all behind those dark eyes, locked behind a thousand doors, each as opaque as the next. What would it be like to get behind them? Maybe I'm only now resigned to the idea that I won't ever know.

His bed is just as modern and impersonal as the rest of the condo, a low-slung floating platform that feels like a boat adrift on the ocean. That's where I curl up beneath a heavy down comforter. The pillow smells like him, something ineffable I recognize even if I can't name it, and I drift asleep to the comfort of it.

CHAPTER TWENTY-SEVEN
Hollow Victory

THE SHINE OF the boardroom table reminds me of the flat white of canvas. It's a place with promise, where something can be made that wasn't before. Money, usually.

The first time I was here I was too busy being pissed at Christopher to appreciate the room. In the half hour that Sutton makes me wait for him, I have the time to study the cherrywood table that matches the walls. Made from the same trees, I think. I have the sudden sense that they were built by hand—by Sutton's hand. That he sawed and sanded these boards. Put whatever this glossy stuff is on top so a sheet of paper can fly all the way across, no friction, all inertia.

There's a kind of romance to that idea, that he would have carved this boardroom himself.

He's angry at me, something I would know even if he hadn't given me the message through the receptionist that he would be handling an important phone call before joining me. Even if he didn't enter the room with his blue eyes flashing and his body vibrating with tension.

I would know he's angry because of the way I left him. The way I chose Christopher. At least that's how it would have seemed to him, and maybe that's how it is.

He drops something on the table, and just like that, it glides a little. Magic. "Our construction permit which has been on hold for two weeks, finally got reviewed. And denied."

Of course it did. We pissed off some of the most important people in the city last night, as well as each other. So much for diplomacy. "Did you by any chance make this table yourself?"

A frown. "Safety concerns, at least that's the claim. I figure if we address them, they'll just come back with something else. The reasoning is just a technicality."

"Because I have to wonder, if you *did* make the table, then you must have made the walls. And who does that? Making walls with their bare hands?"

"We had the construction crew on hold while we tried to push through the review, and now we're going to have to tell them to wait longer. Indefinitely, maybe. Are you going to actually discuss this with me or just talk about the damned walls?"

"The transportation of walls has become something of a personal interest."

He wants to say something about the construction crew that will no doubt be important, but he looks over at the wall and blinks. "You move walls the same way, whether you make them yourself or not. With a truck."

And that wraps up Sutton in a single sentence. *With a truck.* Something idealistic enough in him to want an office built by his own hand. And something practical enough not to wonder how it will be done. The grin on my face, I couldn't stop it for anything. "You're amazing."

He studies me. "Did you and Christopher keep drinking all night?"

"Slept like a baby, even though his mattress is hard."

As soon as I say the words, Sutton's blue eyes turn to frost. I wish I could take the words back, or explain that we didn't do anything, that Christopher wasn't in bed with me. Except that there's voices coming from the reception area. And then Christopher stands between us.

"Good morning," he says, his gaze detached and his suit impeccable.

He was gone when I woke up this morning,

leaving me in his apartment. There was a cup of lukewarm coffee on the counter made with sugar and extra cream, exactly the way I drink it, which was the only sign that he knew I was even there. I ordered an Uber to L'Etoile, where it took a very long shower to feel human again.

Somehow Christopher went from melancholy drunk to determined in the space of a few hours. It's like there's a magnet between him and this focused businessman. No matter how far away he slides, he can snap back in a second. He drops a finger on the permit and draws it toward him, reading without expression.

Sutton strolls over to the far corner, where he runs a hand over a knot, his touch familiar and almost caressing on the wood. He would touch cherished skin that way. "We'll need to appeal," he says.

"Yes," Christopher says, pushing away the paper, letting it slide. "It won't work, of course. And we don't have much time if we want to stay on schedule."

"Seems unlikely," Sutton says, but he adds, "There are a lot of men counting on that income. Would be good to come through for them."

"There's a domino effect with getting construction and our contracts with retailers."

"And we would be in a stronger bargaining position when the construction crew inevitably tells me it'll take longer. Hard to make the point we're in a hurry if we're slow as mud."

Christopher nods. "So we're agreed."

I'm not sure what they've agreed to, except that having their construction permit denied is a bad thing for many reasons. I could have told them that. Then they look at me, and I realize that I'm going to play some part in getting this resolved. That's only fair considering it's the reason why I'm here, but I'm going to need more than clipped words.

"Mrs. Rosemont was *really* mad, you guys."

Christopher gives me a half smile. "I'll go to city hall. I have a few contacts there I've been working. A few angles that might help this go through."

"Bribes?" Sutton asks.

"It looks like we'll need them. Which means we don't have money for those thousands of book restorations and moving the damned wall. Corruption doesn't come cheap."

"Wait." But I've already lost control of the situation. I lost it last night when the first punch was thrown. Or maybe I was foolish to think I could control men like this.

This was also supposed to be the ticket to my mother getting the experimental treatment. That money will go to rich men instead, making them richer. Which strikes me as completely ordinary, all of a sudden. That's how things have always worked in our lives.

Christopher looks at me, seeing right through all my worry. His eyes soften a fraction. "You did the work we asked you to, better than I could have predicted. I'm the one who fucked things up. Your mother isn't going to have to pay for that. We'll pay for the butterfly garden."

He's probably right, being a bastion of ethics and correctness. It still feels like a hollow victory. I don't want to take money they need for construction. The only thing I ever wanted was to spend the money I already had. I never should have agreed to stay here.

Christopher's forehead furrows. He doesn't say anything, though. Nothing to reassure me. And he certainly doesn't offer to let me use the trust fund.

"I'll call Victor and the construction guys," Sutton says. "Try to work out some kind of contract negotiations so they don't walk away and start another job."

Christopher nods and leaves without a backward glance. I watch the back of his head as he goes, those broad shoulders, the determined way he leaves, like a man going to war.

Sutton doesn't look at me either as he sets up a meeting time on his phone.

For two men who couldn't pay enough attention to me last night, they sure are avoiding me in the morning. It doesn't do nice things for a girl's self-esteem.

"Our fault," Sutton says, sensing my guilt.

They fought over me. Does that make it their fault? Or mine? We were so close to having the society's approval. "The table is beautiful," I tell him, touching the smooth edge of it with my forefinger.

His blue gaze follows my touch. "Yes."

It's not beautiful like Medusa with her blue-green lips and serpent hair. She tried so damn hard to be understood. Wanted that more than anything, but the men she spoke to kept turning to stone.

The table is different. It doesn't need to say anything. It just *is.* Like the earth and the sun and all the vibrant things in between.

"I just keep thinking... why didn't I see this when I came here the first time? How beautiful the table is and that you must have made it yourself."

"You didn't know me then."

CHAPTER TWENTY-EIGHT

Battle Strategy

THE FOUNDER OF L'Etoile was a woman who called herself French royalty, but rumor is that she ran a brothel in Paris. Maybe both of those stories are true.

It makes me wonder if every old building has some dark sexual secrets, irreverent to the beauty of the place. Maybe there was a deviant sex club that met in the library after hours. I could look through those shelves for months, for years, and not uncover every secret the building holds.

I won't be here long enough to find out.

Christopher managed to push through the permits with bribes and threats and who knows what else. The books are going to be dragged to the landfill, the carved wall torn down like plaster.

I'll be on a plane out of Tanglewood before it happens, because I can't stand to watch that kind of beauty destroyed. Not like I'm doing them any good here anyway. I may as well go back home, where I can at least make sure Mom is eating proper food instead of whatever berries-and-twigs diet her herbalist has come up with.

Maybe it will be as useful as the experimental treatment I didn't get her into.

A knock comes at the door while I'm packing. So they got my awkward little resignation text, the kind you send when you were never really working for someone in the first place. It's tempting to pretend I'm not in the room, but I'm a grown-up, damn it.

Besides, a perverse part of me wants to say goodbye. Even without knowing whether it's Sutton or Christopher—I want to see whoever's on the other side of the door one last time.

I open the door, and Sutton stands there looking like sunshine, vibrant and so bright it's hard to face him. A half inch of scruff from a long day of work, some of it spent in the sun. Hercules in the flesh, powerful and unreachable and just a little bit mortal.

"Did you come to say goodbye?"

He prowls into the room. That's his answer, but I already know he didn't come to say goodbye. This isn't the kind of man to break my heart and make it easy to leave. Is that what I find so appealing about him? Or maybe it's the way his muscled body looks in a suit. Hard to say. There's a lot to love about Sutton Mayfair, for some other woman. Some woman who doesn't have a plane to catch tomorrow, even if it makes my stomach drop to think about.

His blue gaze lands on my suitcase and then moves away. An obstacle, to a man who must take pleasure in tearing them down. It's strange that I'm hoping he succeeds even while I steel myself to fight him. That's the kind of perversity that comes from having parents that loved and hated each other. From being the rope they tugged back and forth for almost two decades, leaving me frayed at both edges.

I might hate the way Christopher pushes me away, but at least I'm used to it.

"How's your mother?" Sutton asks, throwing me off guard.

That's probably on purpose. Some kind of battle strategy. Make her think you care about her. Then do something terrible. "I talked to her this morning. She tried to make a kale smoothie but forgot to put the lid on the blender, so it sprayed everywhere."

His gaze meets mine, so direct and clear it steals my breath. "I thought that might be why you're leaving. If she weren't feeling well."

"She's doing great," I say lightly. "Kale is a

cancer killer."

He watches me without a change in expression.

"That's what her herbalist says." And suddenly it's too personal to talk about, vegetables and remission and the sinking fear that I'm going to lose her, too. That's when I'll be all alone. When you're forever held taut from both ends, the most scary thing is to be let go.

Steady blue eyes seem to know that. "There's unfinished business between us, Harper. It's not over because you sent a text message."

He doesn't ask me to stay. Maybe he knows that would make me run faster.

"I'm sorry if you thought…" I have to clear my throat, pretending to be stern and unfeeling. I'm playing a part right now. The part of Christopher. "If you thought there was something between us. It was just a little fun. A little…kissing."

My denim shorts might as well be made of flimsy lace, my black tank top completely see-through. That's how it feels when he looks down my body at the places he touched. At the places he kissed—especially between my legs.

His gaze lingers there, and I turn liquid. It's a travesty to call what he did to me *kissing*. He turned me inside out. Made me feel golden and silky and hot. There's alchemy in his fingers and his tongue. He turned me into a river of precious metal.

That was before I sent him a text that said, *Thanks for the memories, but I think it's best for all of us if we part now. PS. I'm keeping the library book.*

He settles on the edge of the high, lace-trimmed bed. It should be incongruous, a rough man against something so delicate. It should be ridiculous, instead of like he belongs there. "Do you know, I thought you were in love with Christopher? When I first met you?"

My throat is suddenly dry. We can invest money and destroy buildings. We can change the landscape of a city, but God, not talk about our feelings. That isn't how it's done.

Sutton doesn't care how things are done.

"You could have asked," I manage to say, my voice only a little shaky. "I would have set you straight. There's nothing between us."

He laughs, the white of his teeth bright in the quiet shadows. Only a small lamp on the nightstand lights the room, and it can't compete with Sutton. "There's something between you. But it's the same way you couldn't see the table and the walls. You didn't know me then."

And he knows me now.

I'm afraid to ask. It's really better if I don't know the answer, if I only wonder and worry forever, but whenever there's trouble, I have a way of falling into it. "So what's between us?"

"Oh, lots of things. Probably love is one of them. Hate, too. Those things go together more than they should. But damn, there's a boatload of chemistry between you two."

There's chemistry here, crackling in the air between Sutton and me.

"We've never—"

"Of course not. Anyone can see that. Christopher wouldn't be walking around trying to tear apart the world with his bare hands if you had. Only a certain amount of denial feels good. The rest just fucking hurts."

I lick my lips, and his gaze tracks my tongue. "Which one was the hallway?"

Only then do I realize I've been walking toward him, walking closer without realizing it. Almost two feet away right now. He's a burning sun, and I've been cold for so long.

"It hurt," he says, soft and almost dangerous, "reading the text."

He isn't diminished by telling the truth.

That's a trick I'd like him to teach me. It doesn't make him seem weak, that he's been hurt. Not with his shoulders this broad and his hands this scarred.

It makes me seem powerful, instead.

Powerful enough that I can reach out and touch him—the backs of my fingers against the scruff of his cheek. Soft when I stroke down. Prickly when I push back up. There's terrain to be explored, to be tested against the will of my body.

My voice comes out a whisper. "I think you did come to say goodbye."

Not with words.

His eyes tell me no, that he's not giving up on this, but his body leans into me. That's something you don't think about, that the sun doesn't just burn. It wants to warm you. I let my hand fall to the angle of his jaw, to the place where his shirt opens and reveals bronze skin.

I close my eyes, letting myself feel the joy that threatened when I heard the knock. If I'm honest with myself, there had been joy when I sent the text—thinking he would come for me. Hoping he would. If I could believe in love and trust and sex, if I thought any of it could last, I would have done more than hope. I've seen where it leads, and I don't want to do that to him.

Maybe we can have one night.

You don't face a lifetime of humiliation and hurt after one night, do you?

His eyelids are heavy now, because he knows what happens next. Some part of him came here to do this with me, because it might be the last chance. It could be the last time I see him, which makes my chest hollow out. That's the empty space where promises could go.

He hooks two fingers in the waistband of my shorts, bringing me flush against his body. My stomach sucks in and then out, in and out, in and out, sensitive skin brushing bare knuckles. "Are you nervous?" he asks, his voice calm and deep.

It makes me laugh, how un-nervous he seems. I'm made up only of nerves, strung together with dreams and desire and a penchant for trouble. "We're going to do it in a bed, after all."

A small laugh. "To spice things up," he says, echoing me.

The words seem less like a joke now. More prophetic. The library counter had been spontaneous and wild. This is different, almost unbearably intimate.

This close I can see the pale striations set into his blue eyes. I could dabble in a thousand shades of blue and never capture them on canvas.

With a sharp pang, I know that I'll keep trying anyway.

It will be my new life's work, this sky.

I don't see him move. We're too close for that; I feel him shift against me. Then his hand cups the back of my neck. His lips meet mine. I suck in a breath, drawing the scent of him into my body. He uses the moment to part my lips. There is no coaxing, no preamble. His lips bite over mine, telling me exactly how our bodies will move. His tongue presses inside, insistent. *Gentle,* his mouth tells me. *I'm going to be gentle with you.* His hand tips my head back, making it easier for him to reach, keeping me from going anywhere. Gentle and implacable.

It's like we never stopped that night in the hallway. This is what could have happened after, his tongue still salted from my body. His hand cupping my breast, his thumb and forefinger finding my nipple. A squeeze, enough to make me gasp. And harder, to whimper.

"I want you naked," he murmurs against my lips.

He's already had me with my skirts around my waist, leaning back against wallpaper. And he's had me bent over a library counter. It's more revealing to let him draw the black tank top over my head. There's nothing underneath. No bra. Only my skin, flushed with arousal. My nipples hard and ruched from the way he touches me. I jump when those calluses brush the smooth curve underneath. It doesn't stop him. He does it again, to see the way I move.

"I—I want—" I don't know what I want, only that it hurts. Is this the good hurt he was talking about? It's not exactly pain. It's more like I'm going crazy.

"I'll give it to you." He bends his head to my breast, using his palm at my lower back to pull me toward him. His lips on my breast make me jerk—not away. I move closer. And then his lips close on my nipple, wet and hot and somehow bright. A cry comes out of me, a high pitch, a keen that makes the hair on the back of my neck stand up. It sounds like grief, but it feels like heaven. He runs his teeth against my sensitive skin, and I gasp.

What a terrible deception. That he would give me what I wanted, but it only makes me want more. Is this how he feels about money, about power, always needing more?

A knock at the door makes me jump out of his hold.

He lets me. That's the only way I could have gotten free of those hands that have held wood larger than my body. His eyes narrow on mine, not even glancing at the door. "Tell me you have room service coming."

I shake my head. "It could be Bea."

Except she would have called before coming down. Or invited me up, if she knew I was planning on leaving Tanglewood in utter despair, for her to comfort with wine and a fancy cheese plate. Hugo really does make the best cheese plates.

"Stay here," he says, curt, like maybe it's his hotel room instead of mine.

"I can answer the door," I say, except there's a cool breeze on my breasts. I'm not wearing a shirt, which is probably a good reason not to greet visitors right now. The black tank top somehow disappeared, so I grab a pillow and hug it to my body, facing the door.

Sutton opens the door and faces the newcomer with no surprise.

From the angle I can't see who it is, but I know based on the low, angry voices that come next. From the cadence of the voice and the rumble of sound. From the excitement in my chest.

"Let him in," I say, because I don't want another fight.

Or maybe that's exactly what I want.

Chapter Twenty-Nine

Competition

C HRISTOPHER'S DARK GAZE finds my bare
shoulders. He makes a sound like a hiss. I
could have touched burning-hot iron to his skin
to produce that sound. I want him to see what he
gave up those years ago.

Not enough to drop the pillow.

Sutton closes the door and leans against it,
apparently content to obey me. Even if I said the
wrong command. Maybe that's what he's doing,
teaching me a lesson.

"Is this what gets you off?" Christopher demands, looking every inch the powerful
businessman. This is how he'd be across the
smooth cherry table in the boardroom, negotiating a contract, establishing terms. "You want two
men panting after your pretty little body?"

It feels like the answer should be no, but the
little flip in my stomach means maybe yes. Is that
wrong of me? My desires aren't anything
straightforward and numerical. I could paint

them, these feelings. They would look like Cleopatra, but she wouldn't be seductive and knowing. She would be afraid. *I'm over my head with these men.*

Christopher prowls toward me, and I clutch the pillow tighter as I evade him. It means giving him a glimpse of my bare back, but it's better than being cornered. He keeps coming at me. I keep stepping back, until I hit something warm and breathing and unmovable.

Sutton.

I'm between both men, caught with only a pillow to cover me. Christopher's eyes are completely merciless. He doesn't feel sorry for anything that happens next. When I glance over my shoulder, Sutton looks a little kinder. Enough that he runs a gentle hand along my side, soothing, settling me for whatever comes next.

"What are you doing?" I ask, but it's not a direct question. Not only for Christopher or for Sutton. It's for both of them. For the room, which has closed me in.

"Nothing you don't want," Sutton murmurs in my ear. When he speaks like that, it's easy to see why someone would do business with them. They'd stake their entire livelihood on a hand-shake with this man, his word worth more than a thousand other signatures.

And still my vision wavers, the whole world wavy and ocean-like. Underwater, that's what I am.

"Drop the pillow," Christopher says, and he sounds the very opposite as Sutton. The opposite of reassuring. He's pure danger like this. "Let's see what we're paying for tonight."

A slap on the face couldn't have surprised me more. I step back into Sutton's embrace, holding the pillow tighter. "I'm not a prostitute."

He gives me a cold smile. "I'm not going to leave cash on the dresser, Harper. For many reasons, not the least of which is that you don't need the money."

If he had coaxed me for hours, I would have held on to the pillow. This Christopher, I know very well. This Christopher I know how to fight. I toss the pillow aside, casually, as if I'm naked in front of two men every day. "I wouldn't be a prostitute, even without my trust fund."

Christopher's gaze doesn't drop. He stares into my eyes hard, like he's saying a thousand things without words. There are probably equations and pie charts in his head. "But I'm still going to end up paying for this."

"What does that mean?" I ask, even though I

know. I'll pay my own price.

Sutton strokes his hand down the side of my neck. His mouth follows the same path. No wonder he was able to tame a wild horse. I would have followed him to the stream. Would have crossed the county to keep his hands on me. "You tell me to stop," he says softly. "Tell me to punch Christopher in the face. Whatever you say, that's what happens."

Heady, that's the feeling of power. Addictive. Terrifying. "What if I'm wrong?"

"There's no wrong," Sutton says.

Christopher's lips twist. "If there's no wrong, then there's no right."

I could kill him, this man who was my stepbrother and my former confidant. This man who controls my fortune. Yes, I could strangle him easily and feel relief.

But not before I lose my virginity to him.

"I'm surprised you would share." I could be speaking to either of them, but it's Sutton who could have demanded we never answer the door.

Sutton who could have insisted Christopher go away.

His lips move against my neck, an enticement all their own. My skin tightens beneath him. "Do you remember what I told you the first day? In the boardroom? I don't mind that you have unfinished business."

Make him suffer all you want, as long as you don't go home with him at the end of the night. That's what he said about the gala. Is that what he thinks about tonight? Except I won't be going home with either of them. "Unfinished business," I say, unsteady. "Is that what we're calling this?"

Christopher's eyes flash. "How generous of my business partner."

Words fall like pebbles into a large lake, almost soundless. Deceptively small. "That's what I did with the library, isn't it?" Sutton's voice is low and faintly mocking. "You wanted it but didn't have enough. I helped you do it."

"Helped." Christopher tastes the word, sounding hard and accusatory. He looks at the places where Sutton touches me—one hand on my arm, his other on my waist. His mouth less than an inch from my neck. I can feel the soft caress of his breath. "This is how you help."

"Do you want her?" Sutton says, sounding unconcerned. The way you would ask if someone is having a nice day, polite indifference—you could almost think he doesn't care. If not for the erection hard and throbbing against my ass.

"I've always wanted her."

The words should be sweet. Maybe for another woman they would be, but they only make me angry. They make me furious. Not the snake-hair kind of fury. This is sly and seductive. It ripples along my skin, turning me into someone else.

Someone who turns her face back to meet Sutton's lips.

I start the kiss, but Sutton is the one who takes it deep. It's not a show, the way he licks inside my lips like he's trying to taste my essence. He must find it, because he groans into my mouth—soft, like maybe he doesn't want to make that sound. I bite him for it, because my body is wild and feral and wants him to make the sound again.

Only a small part of my mind listens. Any second now the hotel door will open and close. Christopher will leave. For so many reasons he'll leave. Even putting aside the fact that he never touched me after that night in the art gallery, even ignoring the tense competition between the two men... threesomes aren't something men do, are they?

Frat boys talk about it at school. Two women, that's what they want. Bonus points if they're twins. But never two men, not for ones as confident and commanding as these. They would kill each other, which maybe is the point. This is a gladiator match, and I'm the arena.

The door doesn't open and close.

A whisper on the back of my hand. On my cheek. It could almost be nothing, except that my skin remembers. I break the kiss to see Christopher tracing my skin, not touching. There's an expression of fierce concentration on his face. This man can discuss advanced economic theory like it's the alphabet, and he studies my shoulders, my breasts, the indent of my waist, like I'm a puzzle beyond comprehension.

Those eyes have never been more opaque than now. It's impossible to imagine what he's thinking behind black marble. Is he surprised that we ended up here, after hating each other for so long? Or does it feel inevitable, like every sharp word and growled insult has led to this?

That's what it feels like for me—inevitable. It's finding silt at the bottom of the ocean after a long way down. I knew it must be here, but I lost hope along the way.

He brushes the backs of his fingers against my collarbone. Lower, lower. Skips over my breasts and touches again at my stomach, making me suck in a breath.

He's going to make me ask, this man. He's

going to make me beg.

"Touch me," I whisper.

His eyes meet mine. It's with cold deliberation that he cups my breast. Tugs my nipple between thumb and forefinger. He doesn't blink, not even when I ache and squirm in Sutton's hold.

It's wrong that I'm held from behind by one man and touched by another. It's the culmination of everything we've done, a physical manifestation of being with Sutton at the theater and having Christopher watch me from his box seat.

Everything more intense and surreal.

"Beautiful, aren't they?" Sutton's voice startles me. He sounds casual, as if they share women every day. As if my breasts are a sunset worth mentioning.

Christopher swallows hard. "Beautiful. I've dreamed about them, of course."

"I think a man would have to be dead not to dream about these." Sutton runs a hand up my side and cups my breast, the one Christopher isn't already holding. There are two different hands on me right now. One calloused and square-tipped. The other elegant and strong. It's pure decadence having both of them touch me. Enough to drive a girl insane, the way they each feel so different, with every stroke telling me, *there are two of us, two men, two.*

My hips rock forward and back, reaching toward Christopher and then back toward Sutton. I can't decide what I want, can't decide *who* I want, and it hurts both ways.

They guide me toward the bed without discussing it. They became business partners for a reason. Even so different, there's some part of them that works together. I'm undressed with four hands moving over me, worshipping me, driving me insane.

I'm laid down on the white lace bedspread, my breasts ruched and sensitive, my legs spread by Christopher's hips. He touches me, careful and sure, finding me wet. One finger presses inside. Two. My body pushes up to meet him, finding the rhythm he feeds me, seeking release.

He pulls away before I can reach climax, making me moan my complaint.

"You want this?" he asks, so soft it might not be important. If not for the way his jaw ticks, for the impossible bulge beneath his slacks, you could think my answer doesn't matter.

It was always supposed to be you. I bite those words back, because they have no place in this moment. No place in front of Sutton, who leans against the dresser, looking hungry and benevolent. He's the one granting us this moment. Is this a gift to me or Christopher?

It might not be a gift at all. A Trojan horse, the way Christopher unbuckles his belt with hands made clumsy with urgency, the way my legs fall open against the bed. Enough to destroy the both of us, the way Christopher catches a condom Sutton tosses across three feet.

And then Christopher pushes against me.

His eyes widen. "You've done this before. Haven't you?"

I turn my face away, hiding. A little ashamed. The hand on my cheek is gentle but inexorable. He turns me to face him, his eyes made a fraction lighter.

"Haven't you?" he asks, soft, even though he must already know. My cheeks are burning. In all the imagined times that Christopher Bardot took my virginity, I never had to tell him.

Never had to admit I've waited for him.

"I want this," I whisper, pulling uselessly at his arms where he leans over me. It might as well be pulling stone columns for all I move him. He'll make the decision for us.

He leans down to press a chaste kiss to my lips. It feels like goodbye, that kiss, and I push up from the bed, following him, *begging* him with my body to stay.

I didn't need to worry. He pushes inside me fast enough that I gasp, hard enough that I arch away from him, stunned and stretched. My hands fist in the bedspread.

"Shhh," Christopher says, brushing hair away from my cheek. "The worst of it's over. I'm going to be gentle with you, Harper. I promise."

It's a promise that makes my eyes sting, because it can't be real. He's determined and hard and cold, but never gentle with me. Except he pulls me into his arms, cradling me, holding me still as he pulls back and thrusts again. My mouth opens in lingering pain, but he captures it in a kiss. It has to be a lie, this kiss, so full of emotion that Christopher can't have.

Pleasure surrounds me as surely as the dark water around a stone.

I sink deeper with every thrust and every breath. His head falls to my shoulder as he murmurs, "Yes, God. Harper. Like that. You're so beautiful like that."

Beautiful. He uses the word, but it doesn't feel like he's describing me. Not the way I look, anyway. He's describing the way I feel around him. The way my secret muscles clench and squeeze, fighting the intrusion. He reaches down to move my hips in some specific way that feels only slightly different, until he pushes in again. Then sparks light up a place deep in my body, electricity running to every nerve and making me light up.

A rough sound comes from behind me, and I look back to see Sutton watching us with eyes a sharp crystal blue. They speak of arousal, those eyes, and something else—a secret plan.

A plan, like this is part of his strategy.

Like he always knew it would come to this between the three of us.

Then Christopher thrusts into me again, and I forget to think about Sutton. I forget anything but the feel of this body working over me, inside me, the warm lips on my neck. He tastes my skin along my shoulder. My breast. When he closes over my nipple, I whimper.

"I need you." Three words. The most truth I've ever spoken to Christopher.

His eyes reflect the need back at me. *I need you.* Or maybe I'm imagining that. And then he closes his eyes, blocking me out again. He thrusts again, hard, making those starbursts behind my eyelids. There's nothing to do but pant and moan and feel when he does that.

I'm drifting in a nighttime ocean of pleasure,

unable to find land but not wanting, never wanting it as long as he does this. My nails scratch at lean, muscled shoulders. He grunts and pushes harder, harder. He bends to my ear, the other side of Sutton. And murmurs, so quiet I almost think I'm imagining it. "Please," he says against my skin, more feeling than sound.

This man, so proud and so strong. He says *please* like a man kneeling at my feet.

And I come like a goddess being worshipped, the pleasure fire-bright in my clit and spreading out to my body in waves. Christopher rides my climax with quick thrusts that take me deeper. There's no air here, but I don't need it, don't need to breathe, only need Christopher—and I cling to him. I grasp at him, hungry, desperate, as his body stiffens and pushes, once, twice, and he cries out, hoarse and broken.

Exhaustion makes me collapse back on the bed, my eyes closed. Sleep laps at my skin, threatening to drag me under. God, I can't fall asleep right now. I shouldn't, but my body doesn't understand that. The last thing I feel is Christopher's lips against my forehead, like a benediction as I sink into sleep.

CHAPTER THIRTY
Animal Pride

W HEN I WAKE up, it's still dark in the room, no beam of light from between the two heavy drapes. There's a warm body underneath me, muscles waiting. My hand clenches in springy hair on a broad chest. Before I look up, I know it's Sutton. A slice through my chest, realizing that we're alone in the room. Sometime after taking my virginity, sometime after kissing my hair, he walked away. That's what he always does. He probably has some academic reasoning in his head about how it's actually protecting me, walking away, instead of breaking my heart again.

"Morning," he says softly.

"Christopher?"

"He left. Are you feeling okay?" He means the virginity thing, which I want to brush off as nothing. Not a big deal. Only a social construct, except it feels distinctly physical right now. There's a dull ache between my legs, a reminder of where Christopher has been.

Beneath a white sheet I can see that Sutton's hard. "I'm fine. What about you?"

A flash of teeth as he smiles. "Don't worry about me."

I'm worried about the way Christopher interrupted us in the hallway. About the way he interrupted us last night. We must have reached the part where it hurts him.

My palm brushes over the muscled ridges and flat plane, down to where his arousal burns against my hand. He sucks in a breath when I grasp him with my fist. This part I've done before, playing in the basements of boys I could barely remember after the fact. They weren't as big as Sutton Mayfair. Not nearly as controlled either. He lets me stroke him, down and down, the rest of his body still like a predator coiled to strike.

"You're sore," he says, his voice like rocks grating against each other.

"Not," I say, which is a lie. It doesn't matter, this ache between my thighs. I want to feel Sutton; maybe more than that, I want him to feel me.

He looks like he's about to argue the point, and God, he could prove it. If he touched me between my legs, I would probably flinch. So I press my lips against his chest, to the side, lips open and teeth grazing him. His body jerks, no longer controlled.

"Damn," he mutters.

"It's just the two of us," I whisper.

It's just the two of us, which means we can finally get this right. Now, when I'm still fragile and sore from Christopher, it might finally be enough to free me from wanting him. If only I could want another man. If only I could want Christopher and have him, that would be enough.

He holds himself back, but only barely. Those muscles that look handsome beneath his suit have turned into something far more feral. He's part animal now, vibrating with need. "Shouldn't touch you like this. Should give you a break."

The memory of those blue eyes watching Christopher comes back to me. He was trying to prove something letting him be the first, but I don't know what. That he might be first, but Sutton would be last? I don't know what he's playing, but there's far too much thinking in it.

So I let my thumb brush over the tip of Sutton's cock, smoothing precome over the blunt satin of him, feel the shake of his body—and the moment when he breaks.

Firm hands grasp my body and turn me over, facing down. I pushed him toward this, but it's still a surprise to feel him arrange me, knees beneath my body, a pillow supporting me. He pushes inside me without preamble, and I'm glad I can hide my soft cry of pain in the mattress.

"Harper," he says, his voice rough-edged with desire.

"I'm okay," I manage to gasp, because I'm stretched and aching—but I'm telling the truth. I can survive anything to feel Sutton come apart. "Please, Sutton. I want you."

He groans his surrender, covering my back with his body. "Christ."

His cock pushes against the walls. He's thicker than Christopher was, or maybe I'm just that sore now, but either way I wince with the effort to let him in. Until his large hand delves beneath my stomach and between my legs. He finds my clit with rough fingers, his touch knowing and merciless. He pinches me hard enough to distract me from the stretch. Hard enough that I'm pushing back so he'll give me more.

"You're incredible. Do you know that? You're a goddamn miracle and you walked into my office. How could I not want you? How could I not have you?"

I'm glad I don't have to answer those questions, because I don't know. My lips can't form words when he fucks me hard and fast, letting the desire from last night build, pull us into climax. His body uses mine in a way that feels primal. A sharp pain on my shoulder. He bites down hard, which sends me over the edge. Orgasm clenches my body as he rides toward his own release. In the last minute he pulls out and spills, hot and thick at the small of my back.

My body collapses, slick with sweat and arousal and come.

Sutton strokes a hand down the side of my thigh, a caress that says what words can't. How I've pleased him. How he needed that and I gave it to him. There's animal pride in me, even as I lie in a limp puddle on the lace bedspread.

There's running water and then he's back with a warm washcloth. He cleans my back and then turns me over, tucking me into bed. My eyes are closed when he joins me, curling his body around me as if he can protect me from morning. As if he can keep me when it comes.

His breathing evens out, and I know he's asleep. But no matter how tired I am, I'm not going to fall asleep again. I'm wide awake in his arms, counting down the hours until I'll slip away. It was everything I wanted it to be—sensual and mind blowing. I'm halfway in love with

Sutton, lying here, but the sad part is, I'm still in love with Christopher Bardot.

Somehow I've only made it worse.

Chapter Thirty-One

A Complicated Man

W HEN I WAS little we had a series of condos in Beverly Hills, because Mom wouldn't consider living anywhere else in LA. Maybe it's because I grew up with her that I could never condemn the rich. It was taught to her the way other families tell their children to say *please* and *thank you,* the idea that you were defined by the zip code you lived in.

It wasn't only pride. It was life or death.

I understand that survival instinct, because she taught it to me.

There would be some new husband, always. Our refrigerator would suddenly be full again. That's how I knew it was happening. He would pay the bills that were overdue. He would pay out the lease so we could move in with him. All these things were so normal I didn't know there was any other way to find food or shelter.

Maybe art saved me, because talent is the great equalizer. There's no way to pay for more of it.

No way to trade a roll of cash for the hours spent late into the night, working and tearing your hair out. It was the whisper in my ear that there's something else that mattered.

In the end even art could not defy that survival instinct.

Those paintings supported us after Daddy died. They paid for the two-bedroom condo in Baldwin Hills. There are ceramic picnic tables in the courtyard with mosaics of palm trees etched into them. Our window overlooks the parking lot.

Absolutely no one from our old life would speak to Mom if they knew she lived here. But then, they never spoke to her again after the public humiliation of the will came out. It was as bad as we thought it would be. Worse, because of the memes and public jokes that came after. We were a spectacle for a couple weeks, before another rich person did something crazy.

"You look skinny," she says, puttering around the small kitchen. Nothing that tastes like food has ever been made there, but we manage to eat well enough on premade bags of salad and delivery from the Korean restaurant down the street. "I'll make you something to eat."

"Not hungry," I tell her, dropping my luggage in the middle of the living room. I left Sutton warm in my hotel room and took the first flight out of the airport, that's how desperate I was to leave. Then I caught a connection to LAX. "Besides, I should be the one making you something. Tell me you've had more than smoothies."

She comes and sits down by me, holding a glass of green sludge. "I think it's helping. I haven't felt this good since the treatment started."

I peek at her through one eye, but she looks serious. And peaceful.

It's a little ironic that the will reading was probably the best thing that could have happened to her. She lost everything that mattered to her that day. But once we picked up the pieces, she didn't have that frantic edge.

And she never again had to sleep with some new husband to fill the fridge.

"I was thinking of starting work at the studio again," she says, referring to the yoga studio. She started working there maybe a year after the will. She teaches classes or works behind the desk. They basically pay pennies, but it helps her feel in control of her life.

"The doctor said you should rest."

"Doctors," she says, waving away cancer like it's nothing. "I feel fine."

She doesn't look fine. There are still shadows under her eyes, but they aren't as pronounced as before. I can't look at her and not see the way she looked in that room full of her enemies. That day may not have broken her, but it broke something in me.

Impulsively I reach over and touch her hand. She looks surprised. Then she folds me into her skinny arms, resting my face against her shoulder the way she did when I was little.

"What happened?"

Only two words, but they have the power to make me cry. Maybe because there's already such knowledge in them. Out of anyone she knows what it's like to be hurt by a man. I let the tears fall, because love is terrible, terrible, terrible. And it doesn't go away.

When I can speak again, it isn't Christopher that I talk about.

"Sutton walks around like nothing can surprise him, like nothing can shake him. He's so freaking capable, it's like vibrating in him. It would be just a day's work to make a business deal and then build a house."

"I see," Mom says, in this speculative voice like maybe she *does* see. Maybe her motherly instincts have somehow told her that her daughter had a wicked threesome in a French hotel.

"But I left, and worse than that, I think I let him down. He wanted me to save that library. He never told me that, not with words." He spanked me with a nonfiction book over the counter, though. "It's something I felt from him."

"Wasn't it his company?" she asks. "He could stop the construction if he wanted."

There was that story about the horse, though. About Cinnamon. You didn't throw away a horse because it was wild. You kept it, even when you weren't sure what to do with it. And then one day someone came along, someone no one expected, to tame her.

That old library lives and breathes as much as any animal. Christopher doesn't feel that. For all that he genuinely cares about me, he sees the building as a commodity. Real estate.

"I think maybe... finding me was his way of stopping the construction."

It meant he put his faith in me. There's a knot in my stomach that says I let him down.

And I let that old library down.

"I didn't get you into the treatment study."

"And I didn't want to do it. I would have, for you, but I didn't want to." She would have put herself through the pain of needles and chemicals, because I want her to get better. Does that make me selfish or stupid? Maybe both. Or maybe I'm just a little girl who wants her mother.

"Daddy would have paid for the treatment," I say, feeling stubborn.

"Yes," she says, simple and certain. "He would have insisted that I do it, too, even if I didn't want to. You and he are a lot alike."

"I don't know whether that's a compliment." On some level I've been doing to my mother what Christopher does to me. Using my protection of her as a crutch. She did need me once, the way I needed him to dive in after me and rescue me. But she doesn't need me to make smoothies or buy butterfly gardens in her name.

"Of course it is. I loved your father."

"He loved you back."

"He asked me out, you know. That night at the art gallery. Asked me on a date, like we were young and foolish. I said yes, of course. I could never say no to him."

My throat burns. No wonder she had thought he wouldn't leave her out of the will, among many other reasons. And we'll never get to ask him why he did. Was it a moment of anger toward my mom? Was it a lesson for me? But he didn't have any answers for me.

"Do you wonder why?" I ask.

"Sometimes. Not much, these days. He was a complicated man. Ambitious. Afraid."

That makes me look up at her. "Afraid?"

"Afraid that someone was using him for his money. He couldn't let it go. He never really trusted anyone." She's looking into the past now. "He loved me the same way I loved him, without being able to help it. That kind of love, it takes away your control, and he hated that."

It breaks my heart to think of how different we could have been. If she and Daddy had gone on a date and then another. If they had finally been able to reconcile their love into building a life together. So many possibilities ended the night of that exhibit.

I close my eyes tight. "I think I have to go back."

It was fear that sent me away from Tanglewood like a scalded cat. But I can't wait the rest of my life wondering what might have been. Love is outside our control, but we aren't defined by love. We're defined by our choices. Our actions. By the willingness to do what's right even when it's hard.

I've always been hurt that Christopher didn't fight for us, but how can I walk away without fighting for him? Without fighting for the library?

Somehow those two things are the same.

Mom smoothes my hair back. "You always were my warrior. Even in school, with that Medusa painting. Even when it seemed impossible. You never gave up."

"I gave up this time." The words are acid in my mouth.

"Nonsense. You came home because you wanted a kale smoothie and a hug. That's not giving up. That's taking a break. Everyone needs a break."

"What if I'm too late?" I'm not thinking of the library crumbling, though I should be. I'm thinking of the look in Sutton's eyes. I'm thinking of the way he held me like I was something precious, and the way I walked away. He won't forgive me for that. I don't blame him.

"Well," Mom says, her voice half pragmatism, half mystical acceptance of the world and its vagaries. "You might be. But you won't know unless you try."

CHAPTER THIRTY-TWO
Sacrifice

MY UBER DRIVER is from Egypt, something he tells me only when he sees the library book I'm reading as we leave the airport. Maybe he thinks I'm getting ready for international travel. "Don't use a purse," he says. "Too easy to steal. You want to keep things in your pockets, but deep inside. With buttons or zippers to close them."

"You seem to know a lot about picking pockets."

He waves a hand. "Everyone knows a lot. It's the only way you don't get robbed. There's no place on earth with more thieves than Cairo."

That makes me think of the Thieves Club, the semi-ironic name that four men in Tanglewood gave themselves. Hugo and Sutton. Blue and Christopher. Because every dollar they earn must be taken from somebody else. "Is that why you moved here?"

"It was the killing," he says frankly. "The

stealing I could live with."

"That seems reasonable."

"I have two daughters. It was no place for them to grow up."

Fathers. So protective. There's a tightness in my throat I don't want to be there. It's terrible to be angry at someone who isn't alive to defend himself. The older I get, the more sure I am that he knew what would happen at that will reading. Maybe he would have changed it if he and Mom had started dating for a while, but at one point he knew he would humiliate her.

He did it to protect me. He knew I would hate him for it and did it anyway.

"Don't believe anything they tell you," Abdel says. "They will try to sell you a thousand artifacts in the streets and around the pyramids. Mummified cats, but you open them—only birds and rocks and dirt inside."

"Why would I want a mummified cat?"

"Ancient scrolls that are made of plastic. Convincing plastic."

"Okay, I'd like an ancient scroll. I might have fallen for that one."

"They charge you so much money, that's why you believe it's real. That is the irony. If it was cheap to buy, then you would know."

Abdel takes me to Walmart, because it's the only place that sells paint at midnight. He accepts cash for waiting in the parking lot and helping me load the supplies into his trunk.

Then we go to the library.

"This place doesn't look open," he says, eyeing the dark corners in all directions. "Or safe. This looks like a place you will experience the stealing."

"Better that than the killing," I say, moving the gallons of paint to the curb. There's a lot to do before morning, and I think construction crews start sooner than art gallery exhibits.

He walks toward the driver's side door. Sighs. Comes back. "I don't think I should leave you here. Probably you'll get stabbed and then they'll take away my Uber license."

Clear as day I can hear Christopher's voice telling me I have a death wish.

Maybe I did, back then. It's not that I wanted to die, but I didn't really know how to live. There was always money in the way, always something that had to be fought over. Always a struggle to survive.

"I'll call a friend," I say because I'm a long time from sitting on a railing alone.

On my phone there's a long list of contacts.

People from Smith College who always knew where the best parties would be. Artists from New York City. Actors in LA. There are only a handful of people in Tanglewood. I'm not going to call the newly expectant parents, Bea and Hugo, to the west side in the middle of the night, even if they would come.

Even though I know I can't call him, that I lost that right, it still hurts to see Sutton's name. It would be nice to have his steady, capable presence beside me while I do something inadvisable. My finger hovers over his number, not pressing.

And then there's Christopher, who helped me paint a mural once. I thought I might have fallen in love with him that night, the night he kissed me, but I think it was earlier than that. When he wrote me a letter at my boarding school in Germany.

When he dived into the water after me.

I'm not sure who I am if I'm not the girl hopelessly in love with Christopher Bardot.

Tonight I'm going to find out.

There's no listing for the Den online. None for Damon Scott, either. Finally I have to call Avery who has connections in the city. She gives me Penny's number, but there's no answer. In the end I have to settle for leaving a message and hoping she gets it in time.

And that she'd even want to help if she knew.

Abdel parks with his headlights angled so I can see what I'm doing. He also orders pizza, which is initiative I appreciate in a man. "I didn't drive you around the city for two hours so you could get murdered," he says when I tell him to leave. I'm pretty sure I'm going to send his daughters to college. I'll be past twenty-five when they need the tuition, finally and forever in charge of that damned trust fund.

By the time Penny arrives, I have the eyes painted, which is no small feat considering I'm using a fifty-dollar ladder that had clearly been used and returned before I bought it. It leans up against metal and glass that's decades old, shaking with every brusque wind. My canvas isn't a wall, not really. It's the entire south side of the building. Mostly windows. Some brick.

The eyes are the most important.

Usually that's true in a portrait, but it's a million times more true right now.

This Cleopatra isn't sexy. Isn't seductive. Unless it turns you on to be with a woman who wants to destroy everything you've worked for, which some perverse men probably do.

She's angry, this one. Determined. Resolute.

They paint her knowing, usually. As if the world is full of puppets she makes dance. I think she knew what she was doing but couldn't have known the outcome. It's an act of sacrifice to throw everything you have toward a cause. Part of you has to be sure you'll lose to even try.

Like the way I know this painting will be demolished at six a.m. There's going to be a wrecking ball right through Cleopatra's face. With every stroke of these cheap brushes and clumpy paint, I know it's the best work I've ever done. Art with more than prettiness or pride. Something more important than power.

There's survival, something every woman has had to look in the face.

And sometimes, sometimes we walk into a fight we know we're going to lose.

CHAPTER THIRTY-THREE

#Freethelibrary

THERE'S A CROWD by the time the construction crew shows up. I expect to see Sutton with them, because he's the one who's always managed them. It's Christopher who appears in a suit and sunglasses, looking like he's already made his mark on the world instead of only beginning. He does not look at all surprised by the crowd that's assembled around us.

At first it was only Penny who came and Damon who followed her. There were men who came to consult with Damon, and I wondered whether that was a regular thing. Whether people showed up at the Den at all hours to whisper some serious thing and receive a response. Probably. Eventually word got out, and people started coming to watch.

The protest takes on a life of its own.

It has a hashtag before I even think to post on Instagram: #freethelibrary. Local businesses pick up on it, some of them more serious than others.

Because books are worth saving! posts a local coffee shop.

Mention #freethelibrary to get 30% off, posts a vintage clothing store.

Along with a random ad for shoes.

Blinding light glints off dark sunglasses. He might as well be a stranger, this man in a suit. He looks that cold standing in front of me. Nothing like the man who shivered in my arms.

He looks around before speaking, not in any rush to tell me he's going to destroy this painting. And the library. "Was this a long game?" he asks finally. "You wanted everyone to hate me after the will reading. I think now it's done."

"I didn't twist your arm into buying a historic building, if that's what you're asking."

"It's not."

My mouth is dry from exhaustion and dehydration and paint fumes. He kissed me once, when I was high on the stuff. It won't happen again. "This wasn't about revenge. No. I would have done this for the library. For me." *For Sutton.*

"Are you going to chain yourself to the front doors?"

That makes me laugh a little. "I don't have a death wish. Not anymore."

He absorbs that for a moment. "Sutton isn't here."

"I can see that." His hair would glint like spun gold in this light. His blue eyes would dance with a thousand things to say. His absence is as loud as a shotgun. "He's at the office?"

"Not likely. He quit after you left."

It's like falling two hundred feet and landing backward in the water. Like having the breath knocked out of me. "What?"

"He didn't send me his itinerary, but I figured he would be in LA by now."

"No," I whisper, because that means I'm too late.

"He can't exactly pull his money out. Can't close the barn doors after the horses have been let out, was the way he put it. But he can resign his position. That was him choosing you over money, in case the grand gesture wasn't clear."

There's no air at all in my lungs. No air in the warm morning mist. I'm left to sink and sink, unable to breathe. Unable to think. Sutton did that for me. He left everything—for me.

The grand gesture I always wanted from Christopher... Another man gave it to me. It makes me wonder how much of the world I've been ignoring in my tunnel vision. How much of life I've been hiding from in pursuit of a man who doesn't want me as much as I wanted him.

Suddenly I can't stand to wait a second longer. Whatever threads of love I felt for Christopher Bardot, they fall to the concrete outside the broken library. Gone.

It doesn't feel like a loss. It feels like being free.

Is Sutton in LA, knocking on my mom's condo right now?

Except she would have called me. And he would have had time to arrive if he followed me quickly. Maybe he hadn't come for me, no matter that Christopher thought he would. He might have left for good, the way a sad little boy tried to do with a wild horse a long time ago. There would be no water's edge to stop him this time.

Christopher studies the painting through his sunglasses. "Cleopatra?"

There's a hardness to his jaw like it pains him to speak, and as much as I've fought him, I can spare him that. This painting won't be enough to save the library. Nothing will.

"She knows what's coming," I say, softly so no one else hears.

He huffs a laugh. "As it turns out, Sutton was right. You do have the skills of diplomacy we need. You can convince people to do anything. Unfortunately you convinced them to hate us."

I look away and manage a small smile. "And it turns out you were right. It doesn't matter whether they hate you. You have the deed and a wrecking ball."

"It didn't have to be like this," Christopher says, his jaw tight. There's a muscle that works. A slight flare of his nostrils. The slightest signs that he's upset. He had those same signs the day the will was signed, but he would not be swayed then. Not now, either.

Strange, the way I can admire his resolve even as it tears us apart. "It was always like this."

"You can probably make them riot," he remarks, his voice even. "An angry mob."

"To break the windows in? To steal the books? A little counter to the purpose." Besides the breakfast tacos were too delicious. No one could be in a rage after eating breakfast tacos.

"Or they could form a human chain around the building. It would delay construction, if nothing else."

"And cost you money," I say, gentle now. "If nothing else."

"There's that."

"I'm not going to do that. I made my point."

"Which is what?" He looks genuinely lost. It isn't part of advanced economics theory, what's happening in the streets tonight. It's community. History. These are things he doesn't understand.

"The protest isn't to stop you. It isn't even about you, not really. Protest is a voice for people who have been told not to be quiet. It's the only way we can speak."

I'm not so different from Mrs. Rosemont. We protest in different ways, through the historical society and connections to city hall. Through a painting and somewhat less lofty friends I've made in Tanglewood. Both of us overruled by bribery.

Money has the loudest voice of all.

He finally takes off his sunglasses, revealing eyes that are dark from lack of sleep. It's been gnawing at him, this act. Even that won't stop him. That determination of his is going to break more than the building. It's going to break him, one of these days.

Once upon a time it broke me.

"That's it? You tell me it's wrong and then you leave?"

I look back at my Cleopatra with her sad eyes. She looks resolved to her fate. It's the best art I've ever created. Maybe stronger because I knew it would be destroyed.

Medusa had been different. She'd been angry. Christopher had looked at all that fury and understood it. No, he'd felt it too. The hurt she felt had wrapped itself around him until he felt what she did. If he can understand her then maybe he can understand Cleopatra. It's not rage she feels, though. It's determination in the face of unbeatable odds.

"You could stop," I tell him, one last attempt.

A protest may be a voice, but it's up to him whether he listens. Up to him whether he lets her strength wrap around him. Up to him whether he looks down at me with admiration in his eyes and kisses me like the world could end around us.

He turns and speaks to the men in the construction crew. *Take the day off,* he could be telling them. Instead one man gets into the big yellow vehicle with a crane and a wrecking ball that's taller than me attached. Part of me despairs that Sutton isn't here with me.

That was him choosing you over money, in case the grand gesture wasn't clear.

He should be standing beside me, holding me. It's too personal, my relationship with this library. My relationship with Christopher. As if he's going to plunge that wrecking ball through my heart, instead of the freshly painted face of an ancient

Egyptian ruler.

The construction workers move the crowd back, clearing space for them to work.

It's a random construction worker who climbs into the yellow machinery as the crowd boos and shouts. A mover of levers and knobs. It's Christopher who gestures with his hand. *Begin*, says that hand. From the moment he was bent over his textbook in that cabin, it's been leading to this moment. This moment when he would destroy everything.

A crane extends higher and higher, beyond anything else in sight. Taller than any of the buildings around us, including the library. It brushes up against gray clouds.

My stomach pitches forward. The crowd falls silent as the crane pivots and pulls the ball away from the library. Cleopatra's eyes watch it swing toward her, steady, steady, steady.

The crash might as well be a physical blow. It crushes my lungs and slams into my gut. I'm left reeling, unable to breathe or think or feel anything but pain. Concrete and metal buckle around the ball, which suspends for a moment inside. As it moves away, it leaves a crater so much bigger than its size. Broken wood and brick. Shards of glass.

Cleopatra is gone. Only the shell of her is left—only the outer edges of her sleek black hair, the bottom of her chin. A work that took a whole night to create, gone in a second. It took longer than one night to paint like that. It took my whole life to dream of something more than business and money and power.

It's only by slow degrees that I realize hands hold my arms. They're keeping me back, behind the barricade, which means I must have tried to run forward. I didn't mean to. It wasn't conscious thought. *Survival.* That's what it felt like.

The crane pulls back and swings again. Only a little more destruction this time.

It will take much longer to reach the inner sanctum with the wood counter and the carved wall and the bookshelves. I'm not sure I can watch that long.

The wrecking ball breaks me a little bit every time it swings.

A car pulls up at the perimeter, noticeable only because it's sleek and black and long. A limo, like the kind Daddy used. For a wild second, made uncertain from lack of sleep, I expect to see him step out. *He would stop this.* Except I'm not sure the real Daddy would have. He probably would have invested with Christopher. Only in my daydreams would he help save it.

It's not Daddy who steps out of the limo, of course. Sunlight limns golden hair. Wrinkles shadow a white dress shirt. The crowd parts for Sutton Mayfair as easily as breathing. He has a way of commanding the world without having to say a word.

Even the man in the crane hits the lever to stop the wrecking ball from a third run.

Somehow Christopher is beside me when Sutton approaches.

He holds up a piece of folded paper. "An injunction."

"Let's see it," Christopher says, his words crisp. He doesn't sound particularly surprised, nor does he sound particularly angry. This could be a discussion over the weather. He reads the length of the paper with an impassive expression.

"Turns out the Tanglewood Historical Society had teeth, after all."

Christopher folds the paper. "This won't hold up on appeal."

"Maybe not," Sutton says, accepting the possibility. "But we're done here for today."

Tears prick my eyes. "You're too late."

Sutton looks at the library where there's no hint a painting had ever stood. Through the heavy dust and wreckage you can see the beautiful carved wall, still standing. "We can repair what's happened here. There wasn't any load on those glass turnstiles. Nothing permanent."

It feels like something permanent has cracked inside me, but I force myself to focus on what he's saying. We can fix the front of the library. It's saved, at least for now.

"You did this?" I ask, my voice hoarse.

Sutton shakes his head, slow. "It was Mrs. Rosemont who filed with the court. I gave information in testimony, but it was her connections that made this happen."

"But why... why would you help stop this? Why did you resign?"

Those blue eyes could reach across the entire city, that's how far he lets me look. This man I doubted. This man I desired. He lets me see the deepest parts of him. "For you," he says, simply.

My throat clenches hard. "I wouldn't have asked you to do this. I couldn't—"

"You didn't have to ask. I couldn't be a part of this once I saw how much it meant to you."

"But your investment."

He gives me a small smile. "This one wasn't business. It's personal."

And then there's no way I can hold myself

back.

I launch myself at him, feeling every square inch of muscle on him, made tired from whatever he did this long night. He folds me up in his arms. There's relief and gratitude—and love, in a form more pure than anything I've known before. Love without expectation. Without greed. Without jealousy, which I didn't think was possible. There's clapping and hooting in the background, but all I can hear is his murmured words in my ear.

"For you," he whispers again, fierce.

He may show up with a legal document and a casual smile, but it was no small thing. It broke some principles inside him, the same way that wrecking ball broke some old hopes inside me. We aren't whole people who hold each other. We're each cracked and bruised, but we have each other. God, we have each other.

It's only when Sutton turns again, holding me close, that I see Christopher's dark form against the jarring yellow of the construction equipment. He speaks to the men in quiet terms, his movements decisive and maybe a little stiff. It must have hurt him, this injunction.

It must have hurt him, to lose his business partner.

Did it hurt him any to lose me?

He speaks to me again only when most of the crowd and the construction crew have left. I'm standing in the large foyer of the library, which is quite a bit brighter now that the whole front wall has turned to rubble. Sutton didn't want to let me in—not until they've had engineers to make sure it's structurally safe, but he let me in as long as he stands beside me. There's probably something important about that. He'll let me do anything as long as he can stand beside me. I don't plan to stay long, since I'm quite certain he'll throw himself bodily over me if a brick were to fall down.

The beautiful panes of art deco glass have shattered completely, leaving only misshapen metal in their wake, a skeleton without any flesh. It makes me shiver, looking up at that.

Rocks shift as Christopher steps into the space. He leaves several yards between us. Does he despise me now? My stomach clenches. I care about him more than I want to, even now.

"You've won," he says. "For now. The crew decided to start another job."

Sutton was the good-old boy who convinced them to wait for this project. For all his money and power and determination, even Christopher couldn't make them wait any longer.

It strikes me again that he doesn't seem angry. Remote, is how I'd describe it. That makes me worry for him even more, like maybe he's going through shock. A million dollars is a huge amount of money. Is it gone? Bile rises in my throat. It can't be gone.

"I'll buy the library from you," I say, impulsive.

Before I can realize that Christopher would never accept that, any more than he would dip into my trust fund all these years. That would be unethical. For a man I don't trust, he's remarkably trustworthy.

"No," he says, his voice hard. "Thank you, but no."

Then he turns and walks away, leaving the two of us in the rubble.

There's a sense of loss so wide and so deep, my legs feel weak. My eyes close. Sutton is there to catch me this time, his embrace warm and understanding. I'm not the only one who lost someone. "You were friends," I say, looking back at him. Sutton's eyes are shadowed to a dark sapphire, his brow furrowed.

"We were." There's finality there. "He's the past. You're the future."

And I know he isn't only talking about his friendship with Christopher. He's talking about my relationship with Christopher, which has always been too complicated to define. Maybe it doesn't need to bother me anymore, the amorphous shape of us. It's over now.

I turn around in Sutton's strong arms, tilting my head up. "You're my future."

He pulls me flush against him, and I feel him harden. His lids lower. Electricity runs from the center of his body to mine, making me ache and flush everywhere. "Christ, I want to take you back to that counter and finish what we started."

My cheeks turn warm. "There are still people outside. And no doors."

A low growl vibrates over my skin as he nuzzles my neck. "And strictly speaking I don't own the library anymore, the company does, and I don't work for it. We're trespassing right now."

Something spears my stomach. We don't have a right to know what happens to this old library anymore. We gave that up, along with Christopher. Ironic, because he's the one who wanted to destroy it. There's nothing here but history and potential.

There's nothing here for us right now.

Chapter Thirty-Four
Pile of Rubble

IN THE DAYS that follow I'm alternately called a vandal and a grass roots activist by the local media. The Tanglewood Historical Society invites me to speak at their meeting, which I find ironic enough that I decide to go. Besides, Sutton lives here. We've gone out every night the past week—to Thai restaurants and burlesque clubs. There's no part of the city we don't want to explore, so I might as well put down some roots.

My speech is short and sweet and encourages change through art. There's a small reception afterward with tea and bourbon croissants, which makes me think I might come back to another meeting. If nothing else I'd like to show them we aren't all fist-fights at theatres.

Mrs. Rosemont doesn't seem to hold it against me. She greets me warmly and thanks me for my work in helping save the library. "We thought it was hopeless, near the end."

"I'm glad you had the idea for the injunction," I tell her, sipping the English breakfast tea. It soothes my throat, which feels a little worse for the wear after my speech.

She pauses, looking uncertain. "It wasn't my idea, dear."

"Oh." Sutton must have been modest when he said she filed the paperwork. "Someone suggested that you file the injunction?"

That makes her laugh. "Suggested? No, he wrote it himself. Had the society's name on the paperwork. All we had to do was bring it to the courthouse."

"Sutton can be efficient when he wants to be."

There's a long pause, where Mrs. Rosemont studies her cup of tea as if it holds the secrets of the universe. "I'm not sure I should tell you this."

Unease moves through me. "Tell me what?"

Her gray eyes are soft. "It wasn't Sutton who wrote that injunction and gave it to me."

"Then who?" Except I already know. There's only one person who would figure out the exact method of stopping construction. Only one person who didn't seem at all surprised that it happened. "Christopher."

She nods. "Mr. Bardot called me that night. We had to wake up a judge, which was something I helped with. There were other things we needed—the testimony of the partner, for one thing. Sutton Mayfair was called in for that."

My hands feel cold. And then numb. "I don't understand."

"I asked him why," she says, her voice thoughtful. "He didn't explain himself. I don't think a man like that explains himself very often."

Why had Christopher stopped his own construction?

And why had he hidden that fact? Why signal the construction crew to begin when he knew it would end at any minute? Was he hoping to finish quickly? No, that's not possible. It would have taken too long. And he didn't have to file that injunction. The library would be a pile of rubble and dirt right now if he hadn't done that.

✧　✧　✧

IT FEELS LIKE a betrayal to even stand outside his condo.

Some part of me knows I shouldn't ask this question. This is the railing of the yacht. And beneath me, black water and sharks. Even being here means I might fall.

My arms don't move when I tell them to knock. My legs don't move when I tell them to leave. My body is in full rebellion, keeping me rooted to this spot. I'm the one turned to stone.

The door swings open, and dark eyes widen. Christopher.

"What are you doing here?"

"I came to see you," I say, hiding my nerves behind a flippant smile. Oh yes, I'm used to this. Brushing past him is easy, even with the big box he's holding. Maybe because of it. He can't put it down quick enough to stop me. I push myself up on his granite bar top, swinging my legs.

He follows me more slowly, setting down the box he's carrying beside a stack of others. "If you're here about the trust fund—"

"I talked to the hospital. They told me you approved the funds for the butterfly garden. I told them to name it after Daddy, because it's his money."

Those dark eyes give away nothing. "Your mother's in the trial?"

"We discussed it, but she doesn't want to do it. And I'm okay with that."

He swings away from me, toward the bank of windows. "I have a lot to do today."

"Are you moving?" The boxes already say the answer is yes. Not that many boxes for a nice big condo, but he isn't a man with that many things. That's strange for someone who wants money, who's earned a fair amount of it. It makes me wonder why he wants money, if not to spend it.

He sighs. "I suppose I can tell you, since you're here. I'm leaving Tanglewood."

The news hits me like a wrecking ball to the stomach. "Why?"

A short laugh. "That's a question I've been asking myself frequently."

"And the answer is…"

"The answer is that you'll be more at ease knowing you won't see me around the corner. There's nothing here for me if I'm not going to build a shiny new mall."

"I thought you said the injunction would lose on appeal."

"It will, but by then the construction company will be knee-deep in a real estate development on the other side of the city. That's how these things are played. Timing is everything."

"Timing," I say, tasting the word.

He waves a hand. "It doesn't matter. I'll be out of your hair soon enough."

"Are you going to build your mall somewhere else?"

"Maybe," he says, noncommittal, but I read the answer in the hard set of his jaw. Not right away, because his money is tied up in a building that he can't touch.

"Mrs. Rosemont told me you were the one who wrote that injunction." The words spill out of me like a dam has opened. I'm shaking with relief to have them out. "Why would you do that, Christopher? You're the one who wanted that place torn down."

"I didn't want it torn down."

"Um, excuse me. I think I would remember if you said, 'Harper, let's leave the library up and save all the books and priceless architectural details.'"

"I wanted something new built. That's not the same thing as wanting it torn down."

"It is when there's a wrecking ball involved."

His eyes dance with something like humor. "Fair enough. So it's not going to be torn down. That's what you wanted. So why are you here?"

"I'm here because you lied to me."

One eyebrow rises. "I didn't lie."

"You should have told me you filed that injunction. Instead you told the construction people to start tearing it down, knowing, *knowing* it would be stopped."

His voice is mild. "Like I said, timing is everything."

"You wanted me to think Sutton had saved

the library."

He turns away, and I know I've guessed right. "Does it matter? He did help."

I cross the room and stand in front of Christopher. It hurts to look at those dark eyes, knowing what he's done. Somehow it hurts worse to know he saved the library. "Why?"

"Hell," he says roughly. "You know why."

I don't want to hear this, but I can't make myself walk away. It's everything I ever wanted from him. *Too late, too late.* "Spell it out for me."

"The only reason I was in this city was for you. Because you loved it here, with Avery. Because I thought you belonged here. Turns out you do belong here—with someone else."

"Why would that matter to you?"

An uneven laugh. "Because I've loved you every day since that goddamned will reading. Every day since I dived into the water after you. Probably from the moment I saw you walking up that dock the first day."

My stomach pitches. "Then why didn't you fight for me?"

"Oh, there's a million answers to that one. Stubbornness. Stupidity."

"And at the end?"

"At the end, you wanted Sutton to be the one

to save the library."

"So you gave it to me," I whisper, my heart fracturing.

We're standing only an inch apart. His eyes might as well be a fathomless night sky, deep in the city without a single star. With nothing to guide me. We stood like this in front of Medusa, and he kissed me. She watched us without judgment or fear, the same way the city watches us now.

His head lowers. There's not time to breathe or think.

When his lips touch mine, there are a thousand stars lit up. I'm the one burning inside the open space of him. I'm the one made hot and raging. He dips his tongue against my lower lip, testing me, tasting me, soothing the wild heat inside with a smooth, dark movement.

A sound comes from the door.

It takes me a while to come back into my body from the places I've been. To feel the mechanics of my bones and joints and muscles. To make myself step back. When I do, I can see the door which hangs open behind Christopher.

Sutton stands in the doorway, his blue eyes stark and cold. A lake that's frozen over. There's no way to explain what's happened here, not when I don't understand it myself. No excuses for the fact that Christopher's hand is clenched in my hair. He releases me slowly, finger by finger. Prying himself away. That's how it feels. He takes one step back. Another.

I watch as he becomes the man from after the will reading. I watch as he becomes a stranger. An enemy. "You were just leaving."

There are razors in my chest. They turn against me, leaving only ribbons of wanting, the remains of a pointless dream. "Is that why you were kissing me? Because the only way you can touch me is if you know it means goodbye?"

The words hit their mark, an arrow in the heart of a stone. He turns cold. "Does it matter? You have what you wanted."

Hurt crowds my throat. I cover it up with suspicion. "Sutton?"

"The trust fund. It's your money. Use it however you want. Buy a thousand goddamned butterflies."

He leaves me with that terrible victory, having won control of the fortune that should have been mine, having lost the man who never belonged to me. The man I've always wanted more than he wants me. Sutton turns sharply to give Christopher his exit, careful not to touch him. No punches thrown. That should be a relief to me. It feels like I took the hit to my stomach instead.

I half expect Sutton to storm out of the apartment, but he stands in front of me. Stands with me in the rubble of trust around us, figurative dust floating in the air, the way we were at the library. He's the past, he said then. Christopher's taste is still on my tongue.

"I shouldn't be surprised," Sutton says, his gaze past my shoulder, to the wall of windows beyond.

Words crowd my throat, words of apology, but loss steals my voice. I should have learned this by now, that life couldn't be trusted.

That anything good was only temporary— especially men.

I could say that I didn't initiate this, that I didn't come here for this. That it was Christopher who kissed me. But I didn't stop him. And in my secret heart, I know the truth—I didn't want to stop him. Sometimes a woman has to face a wrecking ball coming toward her with steady eyes. She knows what's coming. That's what I told Christopher. The library might recover. Cleopatra won't.

"I'm sorry." My voice comes out raw. "That shouldn't have happened."

"No? After what we did in your hotel room I don't think I had any claims of monogamy. You can kiss whoever you want."

Those same words might come from a man with no desire for commitment. Instead they're filled with a dark amusement. It makes me remember the glint in his eyes when he watched Christopher take my virginity. The way his Southern charm had slipped for a moment, revealing a cunning underneath. "Whoever I want, as long as you're in the room, pulling the strings. Is that how you like it?"

There's heat in those blue eyes. Betrayal and hurt, but enough heat to blaze like summer. "That's how you liked it, too. I remember how hard you came, honey. Your beautiful thighs trembling. Wet enough to soak the sheets."

My body responds with suddenness, warmth spreading through my body, a wildfire in a dry forest. This isn't the time to be aroused. Sutton must know that. He watches me with that same cunning beneath the surface. It makes me want to toss a pebble into it, to make him ripple. "Why did you come here? Are you following me?"

"It was only a matter of time before you came to see Christopher."

"That means yes."

"Do you want me to apologize?" He drawls the word, making it sound like a mockery. Except he should apologize for following me. And like he said, we hadn't made any promises of monogamy, no matter how shameful I felt to be caught kissing someone else.

Tanglewood is a blade. I'm torn in two pieces, one that loves Christopher. That's always loved Christopher in all his terrible ambition. And one half that loves Sutton, the man of few words and dangerous trust, the man staring at me like I'm the enemy. "I don't think you're that concerned with what I want. This is some sort of game for you, and you've been playing since I first met you in the boardroom."

"You're a beautiful woman. A man would be crazy not to want you."

"Except that's not why you wanted me. It was a competition with Christopher." The certainty makes my stomach turn inside out. "That's why you pursued me from the beginning, why you invited me to the gala, why you made me the offer about the historical society."

Blue eyes glitter. Why have I never seen how much they look like a hard gem? A stone made beautiful and sharp. "You want to question my motives, honey? You're the one who came storming into the office like a woman on a crusade. Looking for Christopher."

The words echo in the air around us. *Looking for Christopher*, he says while we stand in Christopher's empty apartment. "I didn't know," I whisper, my throat burning. "I didn't know that I loved him."

And how for me to realize it, when there's no hope of a happy ending. No solace for me now. No permanence in a gilded world.

Sutton gives me a small smile, this one small and true. "Honest," he says, a little sad. "Honest to a fault."

It would have been impossible to choose between these two men, but sometimes love doesn't give you a choice. The heart has its own balance sheet. It makes its own calculations. I'm the last person to find out what it decides.

I leave the cold, sterile apartment alone, walking down concrete steps to a waiting black car. It's little comfort that I control the trust fund, that I control my own fortune. I'm one of the richest women in the country. In the world. Money can't buy love or trust or safety. It can't stop a thousand pounds of forged steel when it's already swinging toward me. It can't make the pain disappear.

Thank you for reading THE CEO! I hope you loved Christopher and Sutton. Find out which man wins Harper's heart in THE HEIRESS, the final book in the Trust Fund duet…

Ambitious. Intense. Irresistible.

I never wanted to fall for a man.

And definitely not two men.

They tear me apart until I don't know how I'll ever be whole again. Until I'm not sure I want to be. How can I choose between two halves of myself?

The price of survival…

Gabriel Miller swept into my life like a storm. He tore down my father with cold retribution, leaving him penniless in a hospital bed. I quit my private all-girls college to take care of the only family I have left.

There's one way to save our house, one thing I have left of value.

My virginity.

A forbidden auction…

Gabriel appears at every turn. He seems to take pleasure in watching me fall. Other times he's the only kindness in a brutal underworld.

Except he's playing a deeper game than I know. Every move brings us together, every secret rips us apart. And when the final piece is played, only one of us can be left standing.

> *"Sinfully sexy and darkly beautiful, The Pawn will play games with your heart and leave you craving more!"*
>
> – Laura Kaye, New York Times bestselling author

Sign up for the VIP Reader List to get free books, bonus scenes, and find out when my books go on sale:

skyewarren.com/newsletter

I appreciate your help in spreading the word, including telling a friend. Reviews help readers find books! Please leave a review on your favorite book site.

You can also join my Facebook group, Skye Warren's Dark Room, for exclusive giveaways and sneak peeks of future books.

Keep reading for an excerpt from THE PAWN...

✧   ✧   ✧

ONE THICK EYEBROW rises. "What do you want with him?"

A sense of familiarity fills the space between us even though I know we haven't met. This man is a stranger, but he looks at me as if he wants to know me. He looks at me as if he already does. There's an intensity to his eyes when they sweep over my face, as firm and as telling as a touch.

"I need..." My heart thuds as I think about all the things I need—a rewind button. One person in the city who doesn't hate me by name alone. "I need a loan."

He gives me a slow perusal, from the nervous slide of my tongue along my lips to the high neckline of my clothes. I tried to dress profession-ally—a black cowl-necked sweater and pencil skirt. His strange amber gaze unbuttons my coat, pulls away the expensive cotton, tears off the fabric of my bra and panties. He sees right through me, and I shiver as a ripple of awareness runs over my skin.

I've met a million men in my life. Shaken hands. Smiled. I've never felt as seen through as I do right now. Never felt like someone has turned me inside out, every dark secret exposed to the harsh light. He sees my weaknesses, and from the cruel set of his mouth, he likes them.

His lids lower. "And what do you have for collateral?"

Nothing except my word. That wouldn't be worth anything if he knew my name. I swallow past the lump in my throat. "I don't know."

Nothing.

He takes a step forward, and suddenly I'm crowded against the brick wall beside the door, his large body blocking out the warm light from inside. He feels like a furnace in front of me, the heat of him in sharp contrast to the cold brick at my back. "What's your name, girl?"

The word *girl* is a slap in the face. I force myself not to flinch, but it's hard. Everything about him overwhelms me—his size, his low voice. "I'll tell Mr. Scott my name."

In the shadowed space between us, his smile spreads, white and taunting. The pleasure that lights his strange yellow eyes is almost sensual, as if I caressed him. "You'll have to get past me."

My heart thuds. He likes that I'm challenging him, and God, that's even worse. What if I've already failed? I'm free-falling, tumbling, turning over without a single hope to anchor me. Where will I go if he turns me away? What will happen to my father?

"Let me go," I whisper, but my hope fades fast.

His eyes flash with warning. "Little Avery James, all grown up."

A small gasp resounds in the space between us. He already knows my name. That means he knows who my father is. He knows what he's done. Denials rush to my throat, pleas for understanding. The hard set of his eyes, the broad strength of his shoulders tells me I won't find any mercy here.

Want to read more? Find THE PAWN at Amazon, Apple Books, and other bookstores!

BOOKS BY SKYE WARREN

Endgame Trilogy & more books in Tanglewood

The Pawn

The Knight

The Castle

The King

The Queen

Escort

Survival of the Richest

The Evolution of Man

Mating Theory

The Bishop

North Security Trilogy & more North brothers

Overture

Concerto

Sonata

Audition

Diamond in the Rough

Silver Lining

Gold Mine

Finale

Hold You Against Me

To the Ends of the Earth

The Modern Fairy Tale Duet

Beauty and the Professor

Falling for the Beast

**For a complete listing of Skye Warren books,
visit
www.skyewarren.com/books**

About the Author

Skye Warren is the bestselling author of dangerous romance such as the Endgame trilogy. Her books have been on the New York Times, the USA Today, and the Wall Street Journal bestseller lists. They feature powerful men and the strong women who bring them to their knees. She makes her home in Texas with her loving family, sweet dogs, and flying squirrel.

Sign up for Skye's newsletter:
skyewarren.com/newsletter

Like Skye Warren on Facebook:
facebook.com/skyewarren

Join Skye Warren's Dark Room reader group:
skyewarren.com/darkroom

Follow Skye Warren on Instagram:
instagram.com/skyewarrenbooks

Visit Skye's website for her current booklist:
skyewarren.com/books

COPYRIGHT

This is a work of fiction. Any resemblance to actual persons, living or dead, business establishments, events or locales is entirely coincidental. All rights reserved. Except for use in a review, the reproduction or use of this work in any part is forbidden without the express written permission of the author.